THE WOUNDS OF MY FATHER

ROCCIE HILL

BLOODHOUND
BOOKS

For my grandfather, a dour little man with a secret life.

BEVERLY HILLS, 1926

CHAPTER 1

Forty-two years ago today I killed a man, the only person I ever brought down. Already this dawn I've begun to celebrate, uncorking a soothing Skye malt bootlegged to me through Mexico. I will likely down the entire bottle on my own, taking to my chair in the garden and watching the sun rise and fall, and rise once again. I'll pass the day in contemplation of that moment, so evil and yet so pure, dreaming other ways I might have finished his life, perhaps with a knife as he slept or even a large axe. His true end was less dramatic, a jolt from my shooter, the betrayed look in his eyes as he fell, and the sweet slump of his body onto the barleyweeds.

I live now in a dry land by the sea, thousands of miles from where I was born. I've had the luck of reasonable health, save an early malaria and the loss of a finger to a close-range bullet. My career contained diplomatic toil in cities like Odesa and Santander and Milan, where, as Consul, I oversaw relations with our United States of America. The politicians believed I conducted good work during the Great War and the Influenza Epidemic, and I suppose I agree.

My wife and I raised two sons whom we chose to bring to

Beverly Hills rather than the Beverly of my birth. Inadvertently, I doomed them to follow their mother into artistic careers, alcoholic lives in moving pictures instead of diplomacy or even industry. Sadly, my boys will never bring milk to me in the sunset garden, but then again, neither did I for my father.

I was sent to Vermont for my early education. On the morning of my transportation, my mother put me into a private railcar, while I clung desperately to my older brother, Daniel, a decent boy who kept his hand flat on my back for comfort.

"Stay away from children with vices!" my mother hissed, lurching straight at my face. She pressed so close I could smell the morning sherry on her breath, and I strained away, desperate for Daniel's cover. "Be studious and don't embarrass the family!"

When she left, he removed his hand and smiled. "From here, it will get easier." He was ten years old that year, a house prefect already, tall for his age, and good at sports.

During my years at Passumpsic Academy, I discovered the violence boys can do, my stomach and groin becoming the preferred, undetectable targets for injuries. Daniel's broad association of friends often circled around me before much harm could be done, but one year an angry Winthrop with puffed knuckles and an overhanging brow ridge, threw me to the brick and broke my nose. Humiliated and unwilling to report the truth, I withdrew into a story of saving the Dean's cat from a high sycamore branch, a fiction that probably spurred my first career as a newspaper reporter.

By the time I had risen to my teens, Daniel was pursuing more serious studies at Harvard, and the summer before his final year I visited him one last time at college. We sat alongside each other in a plaque of heat in the empty nave at Christ Church, a studded crucifix the color of frogskin hanging high above us. That cross and its sagging Jesus were marked as well with an old bullet hole left during the Boston Siege.

"I had thought to continue on here with Classics," Daniel confessed. "Some very clever men have done this before me."

"That would mean Mediterranean travel, Danny. What a life!"

"Maybe, but it wasn't meant to be. Father wants me to take a position with him in the city." He began gulping the stifling air and picked hard at the skin of his own hand with his ragged fingernails. "His investments are taking him into railroads with that financier, Gould. Not just Erie, but across the whole continent. Down to Mexico, even. They've got their eyes on some godforsaken tar pools in the jungles."

"But you always hated his work," I replied.

Daniel's eyes filled with darkness and the little blue crescent on the vein of his hand ruptured with a seep of blood. I felt myself sinking as we breathed together.

"Should I, though? He spent his life building these industries for our family. Should I refuse him?" He narrowed his eyes. "Summer has been a free fall here. I lost a girl and a future in the same month."

We slipped through the burial ground behind the church and headed for the yard, but Daniel paused, leaning against the stone of our great-uncle.

"Don't let him force you," I said. "Not into a life you'll hate."

"I haven't a choice." He slipped his hand into his coat pocket and handed me a wad of pages. "A contract from Father. Either I join the company or I'm obliged to repay my education."

I unfolded the packet and scanned the top paper. "He could never enforce that!"

"I'm not so sure." He didn't turn away and for a mute, pleading moment, watched me. "Father says the lack of choice makes one focused and strong."

When he traveled up to Passumpsic Academy to visit me in October, we sat under the maples in the fragrant piles of fallen leaves, but his hair was the color of rat fur from the dirt and oils of unwashed days.

"You remember young Hoffman from St Louis?" he asked as he clasped and unclasped his fingers. Without pausing for my reply, he added, "That boy who loaded ships in Galveston. He got himself in a cut-up over wages with the paymaster. He joined the Knights union men. Now he's dead."

My eyes widened and my lips parted, but Daniel kept on. "Father ordered a blanket party for him, and they beat him senseless." He stared at the leaves piled around us. "To death, that is." His lips, blue in the light, pressed hard together.

Through the winter Daniel developed the habit of apologizing unnecessarily to those around him, and while home for Christmas he carried a flask of brandy; at mealtimes he was quiet as a bone. During the first week of January he reported back to the university, and in a light snow on the meadow across from Christ Church, he took his life.

They buried him in the family tombs on the Old Granary grounds. My parents supplied the congregation on the day, a hundred of us waiting in thick fog on the frozen earth while my father and the parson, like dunghill cocks, spoke about my sweet brother's sin. Vanity, they called it, but Daniel had escaped his afflicted life. *Too young to leave a legacy,* my father declared to the crowd, as though scattering lime across his child's body. And when the mist burned away, I cut a branch of holly from beside Daniel's grave, took my mother's arm and left with the others. That thin winter sun will forever remind me of my fearless brother, whose body was one of the last put down in that place.

To my father's bewilderment, when I graduated from Passumpsic Academy and returned to Boston, I refused to further my studies at the Yard. Without notifying my parents, I took a position on the *Herald* writing about city crime and politics. Father allowed this for one year, lobbying always for me to follow the family men to Harvard, but when I rejected that as well as a place at West Point or a tempting European sojourn, he sent me away again, this time to Tampico and the deep coastal jungles of Mexico, the kind of humid, dismal place where even after arrival, you know there is still a good distance to go.

CHAPTER 2

Stories had been telegraphed to my father and his friends about this utterly untouched land, captivating them all with the news of the natural harbor, the sweet and salty lagoons, the timberlands, and the oil that lay beneath. He gathered funds from new investors, and his company planned the railbed and tracks from Galveston to El Paso. When the felled Mexican trees showed disease, Father induced his Boston bankers to lend more money for a new operation to secure rail lumber from deeper in the fog-covered jungles. Desperate work crews plodded through the *chapapote* tar pools, hastily mixing nitroglycerin, downing the trees, and clearing most other life from the swamps, as well.

On Beacon Hill, the stakes in the oil and rail kingdoms were higher and more fluid than I grasped. I remember one muggy day at our home in Louisburg Square, I came upon my father and Gould standing together in the library, two small men both beating their fists on the desk between them, thrashing on about a new case they were fighting through the New York courts. When Gould stopped barking, my father's face had paled to ash.

He bowed his head to the other and nodded. The next week I was on the train to Galveston, followed by a jolting ride on a steamer across the Gulf to the Mexican port of Tampico.

I was sent to work these investments, building American tracks and jetties for the Boston & Mexican Railway Company, before the rainbow turned to mud. As the agent for my father's transactions, I dispensed pay packets to the workers who cut the timber from the ancient pine forests, who dug the pitch and hauled it to the sea.

They were Mexicans, Italians, Huastecos, and Prussians, they were Tejanos I had recruited in Brownsville, and like me, several had traveled out from the Atlantic coast. Stand-offish most of them, smelling of tarry vapors and oxter sweat, they slaved in the swamps for the envelopes of cash I handed them each week. Yet in the evenings when they trudged in heading for the commissary, sodden and exhausted, these hard men would gaze back toward the jungle like broad-eyed boys, incredulous at the bubbling springs laced with oil and the purple hills behind that stained the Mexican sky the color of belladonna.

At first, the water was limpid and sand bars folded right and left along the Pánuco River out to a sea of liquid sapphire. The Alvarado mangroves tangled wildly in these lagoons, slowing progress while my men worked with pickaxes and brute mattocks, all of us coveting the French steam pile driver we had been promised.

We discarded the grease and filings into this water and filled the bay with riprap stone until it clouded brown from the detritus, and until the swamps brought infection to those who worked thigh-deep along the murky shores.

Many of the laborers fell within months from fevers or drowning, and some were buried with their pay envelopes, emptied by scavengers, still in their pockets. When I fell from malaria, I lay for weeks in the company infirmary with the thick, rich smell of rotting skin rising from the cots around me while the mealy ropes of maggots did their cleansing work on my men.

At last, my father instructed the company to pack me back to America, not home to Boston but to a large frontier clinic in San Antonio from where, once healed, I might return to work.

I remained alone in the infirmary of the Sisters of Charity until late May. Neither Father nor Mother ventured to the frontier, paying instead for the skill of Catholics who kept me alive until I could be moved from the halo of their limewashed walls to a fine hotel on the plaza. And there I lay at the age of twenty-six, in smoldering health, devoid of pluck, divining my direction like a fool seeking water until a woman called Stella arrived.

"Would you like me to read you a story?" She sat on the deep oak chair beside my hotel room bed and waited.

A millwheel outside the open window thrummed at us, dipping down into the river and up again, the water so close that I could smell the mud in it. Slowly and with great effort, I lowered my forehead and lifted it again, and as I nodded, the muscles in my neck burned with pain.

I heard the heavy binding of a book fall open, and when she began to read, her voice was earnest and bold. She had brought the Verne story, a long, tedious one about fishes that was of little use to a convalescent, but her spirited voice echoed to me from the surface of the sea, and I listened to her tale until I fell exhausted into sleep. When I awoke the room was silent, and I lay beneath the heavy linen sheet, sweating out another fever made even worse by this insufferably hot land.

The nursing Sisters had told Stella about me, a young man alone and in need of courage, and so she came again the following day to sit beside me through those painful, scorching afternoons, driven hard by her kindness and her own private desperation. She brought salty beef broth prepared by her landlady, spooning it to me slowly. She cupped my chin in her palm, and the sweet smell of heliotrope from her hands rose around my face. When she moved about the room to offer me milk, I almost felt the cool Tampico breezes again, sweet and fresh as though off the broad, blue gulf.

On the summer solstice, she moved me to the hotel veranda in a roller bath chair. A few steps beneath us down the stone entry to the hotel spread the city plaza, and I heard the *bendadors* hawking their trays of pastries and sugared pecans, their shouts rising through the deep, hurling cry of an owl.

"Fresh air will be good for you," she said, piling a pillow at my back, "even if the light is a little harsh."

I waited, breathing slow and deep to recover from the pain at my temples. "Thank you," I said at last. "I've been a very long time in that hotel room." My voice had regained strength, and she inhaled sharply, her eyes wide in surprise. "Oh, yes, Miss Moore, I've healed some, thanks to your kind care. The malaria and the journey up from Tampico only weakened me temporarily."

"The Sisters told me about your fevers. And about the train carriage your father sent to transport you. They were very impressed that he's a partner of Mister Jay Gould."

"A small partner," I replied.

"You've brought quite a reputation with you, all the same."

"Have I? And what reputation is that, Miss Moore?"

"Well," she said slowly, seriously considering my question. "Respectability, of course. Mystery, as well, since the people here are now debating the financial advantage presented by this town caring for the son of Theophilus Ives!" She giggled softly at her own joke. "Most of all, they remember the time your father visited. About a year ago, with secretaries and guards and others, all of them spending money night and day, and for weeks. Our mayor is hoping for another rail line."

We heard the jostle of bridle bits along the rutted road beside my hotel as the Canary Island families, *isleños* as they called themselves, arrived in their carts, carrying tables and chairs and vats of chili stew for the nightly carnival. "Here are the chili queens," she remarked and stood, stepping past me to lean against the railing to watch.

"An odd place," I said. "Squeezed between advancing business and ancient delusion."

Her laugh was infused with warmth and mischief. "You have such a lovely accent."

"I may hail from Boston but I schooled in Vermont. I suspect that's why my accent is strong." Shuddering, I opened my eyes wider to the light. "And you, Miss Moore?"

"I'm only a farm girl from Milam County. Do you know where that is?"

"No," I said. "I'm afraid not."

"Up the railway line past Rockdale." She wore no bonnet, and her hair was dark and glossed by the sun, held up with a clip of carved red carnelian. She had wide, gray eyes the color of mountain fog, and a sprig of damp cilantro lay beside her fingers. "Fine farmland covered with bluebonnets and Indian paintbrush. I was born on that farm." She smiled so easily when she said it, with the confidence of those who have been well loved as children.

"It sounds beautiful. And do you enjoy your time here, Miss Moore?"

She frowned. "Won't you please call me by my given name? Stella."

"Of course."

Having come to town with the heat of May, cicadas the size

of dragonflies rose through the dust clouds and swallowed us in their scratching swells. "They are singing to the death, Stella," I said.

"Just the males, Mister Ives. Just the males."

I laughed at this and replied, "If we are being familiar then you should call me John."

She wore a dark navy dress with a square white collar, and she brushed her hands to smooth the folds of the summer cotton. She seemed a beautiful woman even through my squinting, but the shafts of sun were harsh so I closed my eyes again.

"Are you tired, John?"

"No. Sometimes the light is painful, even at this time of day. That's all."

"Should I push you back inside?"

"No," I repeated. "The quinine causes it. I'll be fine." I opened my eyes but saw little except the slender outline of her form in the virgin shadows. The sun sank faster and faster then, coming to rest on the horizon at the far side of the square where Moorish balconies built of adobe turned from white to pink to indigo in the falling light.

"And do you enjoy this sweltering place?" I asked again.

Stella stared hard at me, drawing in her breath slowly. "I didn't come for the joy." She stood and glanced around the veranda. "I'll find someone to bring you a cool drink."

I had caught her off guard, and she was headstrong. "Sit," I said. "I don't need lemonade. Just talk with me."

She lowered herself back into the chair. "I came to San Antonio to find someone," she said, and the shadow of worry in her gray eyes cradled every harsh edge in me.

"Who?"

"My sister." She opened the Verne book again and took from it a large cabinet card photograph marked with the name of an

artist's studio in Cameron. She pushed it across the table, showing me an image of three young girls. "Lucy is in the middle. We haven't seen her for some time."

The blonde girl at the center was plain, with a round face, oddly arched eyebrows, and nothing of Stella's mignon. On the left stood a taller girl, elegant and beautiful in a simple white blouse and long dark skirt. On the right was my Stella, the smallest of the three, passionate and skeptical and lovely as she stared back unabashedly at the photographer.

"We heard Lucy was here, but I haven't found anyone who knows her, and only one person who thinks he might have seen her." Her face slow-burned to the color of pomegranate blood as she took the photograph again, staring at it. "We were so young on this day."

A cock on the ridge tiles squawked, and Stella turned to the plaza to find it. She looked out past the hawthorn bush and the sycamores, watching some small calves, their backs dusty in the heat, being led toward the west.

"You see, Lucy doesn't want to be found," she said, turning back to me. "The way she left home was not good, in the night after a terrible drama with my father. All by herself."

We sat in stranded silence and all I could think to utter was the useless, "Don't worry, dear Stella. I will help you find her."

She stared as though I had said the words in an inscrutable language, as though I was a dense Narcissus before her, but what was I to do? My education had not fostered me with tools for comfort or care. Passumpsic Academy had taught us to verbalize the basest of platitudes as protection from love, not for descent into it.

She folded her fingers together and laid her hands carefully in her lap.

"Stella," I began, but I had lost her attention and she only looked through me. Frantically, I pressed through the mire of my memory for words that would bring her back, and at last I said this: "I had a brother who died young, so I know what it's like to lose people you love in unfortunate circumstances."

When she looked at me again, her eyes were glassed with tears. "I'm so sorry, John. An accident?"

"Yes, I guess that's what they call it. The end of a long argument with my father."

"Lucy, too. You and I have more in common than I thought."

Boldly, I took her thin-boned hand, warm in mine.

"She sided against her family and she hates us now. All the lying. And she stole from us. She was to go up the territories in Montana with a man, but he was killed and she left by herself. Lucy was curious and wild, but none of us imagined it would end like this." Suddenly, she whispered, "I'm sorry. I imagine I've given you more talk than you expected."

"Not at all."

Her profile was obscured by the shadows, but she turned into the light and said, "This will be a fine night. Maybe you will want supper?" Her skin was pale as a cool moon, and I was half-ready to believe she might love an invalid. "When you are well again will you return to Tampico?" she asked. "Is there more work for you there?"

"As long as there is oil under those jungles, I could have a position in Mexico. Once the rails and jetties are built, there will be shipping. Whether I will return is a different question."

She drew her narrow shoulders up and leaned forward. As she did, I could see the outline of her breasts under the cotton.

"Would you tell me about Tampico, then?" she asked. "I've never been to the sea. My mother used to describe the beaches of the gulf and the water that was so clear you could see flying fish rising up to the surface." She gulped and flushed. "I'm sorry, it's just that she traveled there long ago, when the sea was clean and capable of feeding the colonies."

"Of course, Stella," I said, and giddy with hope, I added, "And maybe one day I'll show you Mexico."

Suddenly across the dusty plaza, the *isleño* men and Anglos heaved and thrashed their fists at each other. Whoops rose through the purple *cenizo* sage bushes as bootless boys ran to watch.

"I was raised on a ranch," Stella said, turning from me, "but I never saw such scenes as these. My father's men were different."

"Don't be shocked, Stella. We are living in a metropolis with all types." She smiled at my irony, and reached her hand toward mine stopping just short of a touch.

Below us leaning against the veranda foundations, stood a stout candy seller, his beaten black bowler covered in dust. He waited behind a deep-rimmed tray filled with packets of coconut sweets, caramels, and salted wild oranges.

"Do you like a sweet taste?" she asked. "I was thinking to fetch us *dulces* before this rumpus gets any closer."

"It may not be safe even now."

"The coppers haven't arrived yet, John. I'll be quick." She stood and moved toward the hotel steps, descending quickly with quiet grace.

On her return, she carried a small sack and hurried toward the veranda where drunken men were now striding across the cobblestones, jostling near her. Stella lurched back, barely missing a collision of the *isleños* and the whiskey cowboys chasing each other callously across the ruddy dirt. The men fell to the road while three white pigeons fluttered up from the hotel galleries, landing high on clean limestone walls.

Our sweets flew from Stella's hands as she grabbed the railing behind her for balance. A tall man toppled to his knees near her, breathing heavily and sweating grime through the dust clouds. He stared at Stella, smiling, and his face glowed red with liquor.

She glared at him without trembling, cold and clear at his wildness, and as she did, the man pushed himself to stand. A tall one, and lanky, too, he swept his long, fair hair back from his forehead exposing a handsome, square jaw.

"Miss Moore," he said, bowing to her even with the turmoil still wailing around them. He stretched out a hand. "You should not be alone on the plaza now." She frowned but nonetheless took his arm. As they moved toward the iron rail of the hotel steps, I saw in his left hand the wink of sunlight on silver, a blade hidden between his freckled fingers.

Quickly, I threw my weight forward to stand, but my legs buckled at the knees and I fell back into the bath chair.

"Stella!" I called to her in a thin, mortifying whine. "Run!" I had no gun at my side, no knife or rope. With all the sad scraps of strength left in me, I heaved forward against the table, and in a deep breath put my hands flat on it, my weight atop them, balancing upright at last. I turned and took hold of the rail. "Stella, he has a knife!" I said, and though I dreamed of shielding her, I could do nothing but teeter and collapse into my chair.

"Of course," he replied easily. "What man would walk out in this town without one?"

At the bottom of the steps he smiled at her again, his eyes flashing the deep green color of the clearest sea. She merely turned her back to him without a word and hurried to me, rolling my chair toward the broad doors of the hotel.

"Are you all right, John?" she asked, leaning down so close her breath touched my brow.

"Yes," I said. "You didn't flinch, Stella. You're a brave one."

When we reached the hotel salon, she stopped and sat on a leather bench facing me. "It's not bravery. I know him. Peter Olenbush. But honestly, there's no danger with him. He's just a rake who likes to bring trouble."

"A drunk, as well," I added.

She lay her hands on the table, the indigo lace of the cuffs covering her small wrists. "He came to my school before. To talk about looking for Lucy. I hired him on, but he wasn't successful, although he believes he saw her once."

"You would do well to stay away from him," I said, but when she looked back at me her lips were taut and I understood I had stepped too far.

Outside, the lamplighters came on horseback and one by one the streetlights flickered alive, *guitarristas* began playing, and the smell of *carne* and cumin spices filled my hotel. We asked for chili and coffee to be brought to us, and as we waited a mulatto boy not more than five years old slipped into the salon and ran toward us.

"Miss!" he blurted, carrying a long stem of deep red myrtle in his fist, which he put on the table before her.

"Rufus," she said, "what are you doing here?"

"Mister Olenbush sent me!" he exclaimed, and the child turned and ran out the side door to Soledad Street.

"Oh," she whispered, but not to me. She took the branch and placed it carefully near her bowl. The peppery smell lay around us, the red petals sharp against the white tablecloth.

"You must not trust this Olenbush," I said.

"He is pressing to court me." She shook her head. "Anyway, I cannot. I signed a contract with the school forbidding relations of this kind. I would lose my position."

I watched her cross her ankles, and the shadows of the dark cotton clung to the curve of her calves.

She followed my stare, and I flushed.

"I'm sorry, Stella."

The evening heat had not yet fallen, and I felt my skull burning again with a new, rising fever. The streetlights glimmering through the stone sills put her in shivering silhouette, while in the trace below I saw the boy, Rufus, watching us eat until I could no longer hold my eyes open. In my darkness, I heard the wheels of a streetcar and the clack of hooves on the cobbles as the trolley moved off the plaza to the north of San Antonio.

CHAPTER 3

*J*une brought the worst season, the hottest, emptiest days when I began to stand, to step unsteadily from bed to pot and back. Still Stella came to me a few afternoons each week, leaving her books stacked on my little table because I had told her I'd been a reporter at the *Boston Herald* and could, indeed, read on my own.

I studied her stories until my temples screamed with pain so I could impress her with my achievement. Sometimes when she knocked I arose with a swagger, balancing myself against the bedpost though my legs were too weak to sustain the stance for long.

We often sat side by side at the window watching the crowds of be-shawled old women selling *tamale* meals on the plaza, our conversation rounding back always to the news in the *San Antonio Light* and its tales of murders and pieties.

By July I had regained my strength, and my father wrote to me insisting I return to Tampico.

We drilled in Tuxpám and have found a

justifiable level of oil. You are needed to
resume your duties.

When I telegraphed him that I had decided to remain in San Antonio, his response was merely this:

NONSENSE.

There ensued a flurry of telegrams from his office, each with instructions for my return to Mexico. *...a fortune to be made!* Or *... don't be delinquent!*

I had expected a measure of irritation from him, or an argument, or delay on the loan against my allowance that I'd requested, but I believed he ultimately would capitulate, knowing full well the gravity of the malaria I survived, since dozens of his laborers had not.

Late one evening as I sat beside the cold dining hearth, a square crystal glass of whiskey in my hand, the night manager presented me with a telegram "From your father, sir," he said. "Just now arrived."

Of course, my father had money in Gould's Western Union Company, and his servants could send telegraphy at any time of day or night from our drawing room. His words were simple:

BE IN TAMPICO FIRST SEPTEMBER STOP FUNDING
UNAVAILABLE TIL THEN

The manager, a greedy Austrian in an unclean suit, watched me. He took my empty glass, his soiled cuffs frayed at the wrists. "Another, sir?" His outstretched palm hovered near my table.

"No," I said. "Thank you." I bunched the paper slowly in my fist.

"Is there a problem, sir?"

A hurricane lamp in the doorway flickered its light wildly across a marble bust above the hearth, and I stood to leave. "Not at all," I said. In the far room of the library the musicians flourished through one last measure before packing away for the night. I looked around and saw that I was the last guest.

The next morning, I stepped out across the plaza, where the sweaty cumin smell of discarded Mexican stew was ripening in the rising heat. I had slept poorly, again and again composing responses to Father's dismissive message. By the time I strode across the little iron bridge to the telegraph office, I had settled for this simple reply:

I CHOOSE TO STAY IN SAN ANTONIO

After discharging my statement, I wandered the river, numb-shouldered and financially embarrassed. I paused above the *lavanderas* as they slammed the townsmen's lye-soaked shirts against the rocks. Onward north, I came to a weedy clearing surrounded by fallen cottonwood logs, where the hot wind and the river light tumbled across the water's surface. At last in silence, I sat on the bank contemplating what I had brought upon myself.

Shreds of ruined cloth lay in the thistles, and probably some pieces of desiccated flesh as well, for this place at the springs of San Pedro was indeed the end of the earth, where descendants of Payaya pig stickers slaughtered their food.

Noises drifted through a copse of oaks at least a dozen yards away, thin, harsh notes from a tin whistle. As the sound approached, I looked up to see a tall blond fellow and small mulatto boy ambling toward me.

"Do I know you?" the man asked. He wore black stovepipe boots, dusty plaid trousers, and a white shirt with a long dark stain down the front. He carried the body of an overly large ocelot, four feet in length, slung over one shoulder and scattering drops of blood as they neared. When he stood at my side, those boots smudged in muck and blood, he touched the brim of his boss hat with a cattle knife and dipped his forehead to me.

"You are Olenbush," I said.

"I'm afraid I don't know your name. Are you the fellow Stella has been helping?"

"John Ives, sir." I pointed to the animal. "I saw one of those at a menagerie in Philadelphia. Hadn't realized they ran wild in Texas. Did you find it dead on the plain?"

Immediately I understood I had insulted his manly prowess. His face tightened and he narrowed his eyes. Turning to the boy, he muttered, "Go on home now, Rufus. Your mama'll be worrying." The child paused, staring at Olenbush, then scurried off down the creekside.

Olenbush faced me once again, frowning.

"I meant no insult, sir. Just inquiring," I said. "I'm quite certain you're capable of bringing an animal down."

He smiled, putting slender fingers to his trim, ginger mustache. "It was troubling one of the north farms. They begged me to make it stop." He tossed the animal over a fallen trunk, its belly fur white in the sunlight, and he sat beside it.

The man had long legs and a long waist, forming a wiry, tight frame. He was stronger, taller, and more handsome than I, with wide eyes and high cheekbones. Where the animal had hung, his shirt was soaked. He opened his mouth wide and grinned. "I thought I'd have the Indians make a hat from it. For Stella."

The animal smelled of waterweed, its pelt damp from the river and its own urine. He had tossed it between us, and as the stink filled my nose and throat, I edged away, brushing droplets from my clothing.

He stretched his arms over his head and cracked his neck from side to side. Tapping the black hat down on his skull, he glanced at me, big and blunt, almost earnest. "What you looking for out here?" A tinge of German melody clung to his words, and as I stared long at him without answering, his smile began to fade.

"A peaceful interlude is all I was seeking," I said.

He lifted the ocelot again, this time curling its body around his shoulders so the legs dangled down on either side.

"You're in the wrong town for that." He eyed me closely. "Stella says you barely survived the malaria. You strong enough now?" I nodded. "Well, come with me back to town and I'll stand you a drink, Johnny."

My skin crawled when he said my name in that familiar way.

Olenbush watched me and waited, at last adding, "You're that visiting gentleman, aren't you? Rumor is that your father owns everything in Boston worth owning."

I shook my head. "That is certainly false." As the wind becalmed, midges swarmed across the river before us, and a gleam that might have been an otter's head slipped along the far bank. "I am new in this town, but not merely visiting. Perhaps on our walk you might point me to respectable boarding establishments."

Olenbush nodded. "Why, sure," he replied. "Sure, sure," and we turned up the path and crossed over the log crowning the berm.

We stood to a free lunch at the Silver King while behind us in the empty dancing hall a Bohemian woman sat before a piano pounding out a polka you could hear all the way to the road.

"Ayla Trinka," said my new friend. "Come and meet her."

A woman of no particular age but nonetheless older than I, she had coarse, earthy skin yet the most beautiful golden hair I had ever seen. She kept pounding with delighted fury, bouncing her head and glossy blonde curls to the rhythm. When I approached and leaned against the upright piano back, she stared bright-eyed into the distance, through those dimmed eyes so deep bluey-green that the day seemed to stop inside them.

I nodded to her, but she did not respond. She looked in the direction of the sheet music on the shelf, blinking occasionally. When she pounded her last melody, Olenbush stepped forward, putting his hand on her shoulder.

"Ayla," he whispered, but she did not turn her head to him. She smiled, but did not move. "I want you to meet a friend of mine. A new friend in our town, John Ives. He's standing at nine o'clock."

This woman, this blind woman, immediately turned her head to where I stood.

"Hello, Ayla," I said. "You play wonderfully."

She began again without responding, gently grazing the keys, her sweet voice taking us back to that desolate place where all music comes from.

"Made orphan and blinded in the mines in New Mexico," he said, "she wandered along the Indian camino, stood on the trace for days and waited. But here she is, hammering those notes. Ayla will save us all."

Didier, the barman, was smacking his lips at us because we drank and ate, and drank again without remorse or responsibility. Old French hack that he was, he provided the best free plates in San Antonio to ensure the men returned to the King and not to the new White Elephant. Oysters, eggs, and yellow cheese were plated across a white tablecloth, even fried elvers that covered the bar with the musky smell of mudfish. Alongside it all was a huge souper of chili, spiced with cumin and garlic by the Canary Island women. All of it salted strongly so to guarantee the sale of the maximum alcohol. Behind and beside Didier, decorating all the walls of the saloon, were paintings, some signed and some not, some copies of famous French and Dutch scenes and some portraits of our earliest statesmen, a vast gallery of haphazard art.

Didier, a tall, thick fellow with long silver hair and tidy gray mustache, pulled out a round gambling board and put it on the counter in front of me. "*Quatre cents vingt et un?*"

I looked at him confused and Olenbush called over, "It's a dice game for drinks. You in?"

"I'm afraid my funds are low," I said. "Until I secure a new position."

"Rich boy like you, I'm sure Didier will extend credit," Olenbush said.

"Didier might but my father is unlikely to do the same. I'm broke. Haven't even got a place to live."

"You never know, Johnny," he said with a loud chuckle. "You might win." He took his place beside me, and winked at the barman as he said, "We'll be needing another round, my friend." Picking up all three dice from the board, he asked me again, "Are you in or out?"

And I, a wide-eyed weakling from Boston, somehow trusted these strangers. "Without a doubt," I said grinning, "I'm in this game."

Just then Ayla began singing once more until next I knew the woman had strung a song of the faraway place where lindens bloom, so sweet and deep that all our betting guffaws were hushed, and we listened awkwardly to her voice glittering across the dim saloon lamplight.

CHAPTER 4

Olenbush pressured me to live west of the river near his own rooms, but I could see those streets were joyless, the deep belly of filth and railroad noise. Reluctantly, he introduced me to Mister Cole, who in turn introduced me to his wife, a deeply irritable, red-faced woman with a fishy smell of uncured river gar. I paid my last pennies for rooms with Missus Cole, the Villa de las Rosas, a simple boarding house neither large nor surrounded by rose bushes.

Still, despite its uninspired appearance, the "villa" was situated near the Rincon Road Freedmen's School where Stella taught the children of our town's former slaves. I dreamed I would see her coming round the corner each afternoon as she made her way to her own boarding house, or that we might take a meal together under the scrutiny of her landlady. Left to my own devices, I concocted an imaginary future of a private school she and I might build together on the town's river, a dream of a vast meadow, happy children, and a stately stone building. Yet so true was Stella to her contract with the Freedmen's School administrators that at first we spoke only briefly, a single lunchtime as she led her pupils to the far San Pedro Springs.

Buttonwood trees grew on the corner then, the last two of a dying plantation growing too close together, with broad deep green leaves discolored yellow by disease. As Stella passed me, the hot winds stirred through the branches and the light scattered across her face. She glanced to where I sat on the veranda of the Villa de las Rosas, her gray eyes wide. The sky was cloudless, the blue of it pale and remote, and the afternoon sun so hot that the railings burned my fingers.

"We're conducting a nature study," she said. Some of the children carried buckets of food and some did not carry a meal at all; some wore shoes and some tramped the road without. Although of different ages and heights, all of them were tied together by a rope at their waists in a chain of giddy, gangly bodies, with the boy Rufus bringing up the rear.

"Wonderful!" I called out. "Science is better than games!"

"I'm pleased you're healing so quickly," she said, leading her trail of roped students off toward Flores Street.

Unlike in Boston where positions of stature came easily for me, the men in San Antonio who owned things did not value my quality education or my name. Instead, my worth was determined by shooting, fighting, and lifting; working with teams of grown men stripped to the waist and chasing hell for leather. I presented myself to Maverick's lumberyard, wearing rough work clothes I had borrowed from my new, indeed my only, friend Peter Olenbush, but to no avail. I couldn't shift planks or tree trunks and was afraid of getting too near the saw. I consulted old Colonel Frost about doing the accounts for his wool business, and close I came to winning that position until he discovered my abolitionist views.

Eventually, Olenbush took pity on me. As a teamster hauler

for the town newspapers, he provided me with an introduction to the publisher of the *San Antonio Light*, and after inveigling the man for a week, I was offered a job writing small, city stories, fielding likely news off the telegraph, and alas, sweeping the shop at day's end. I accepted this instantly before the owner could turnabout, and spent the following weeks combing the wires for events in the far territories that would titillate our readers, including one or two on the subject of my father's most recent Galveston litigations.

Towards the end of the month of July, after an honorable day's work and with the grackles and mockingbirds consorting in the lingering heat above, I was stowing the broom and pan when the door opened and closed again, slow and tight and carefully. Stella stood in the doorway, stamping the dust from her small boots onto the mat. Her back was pressed against the wall, and she held a slender book bound in brown leather. As I watched her, a string of bell-notes floated over the town, an escape of deep, slow cries from the belfry of the Baptist church.

I invited her to sit, and when she moved toward the chair, her skirt and the crinoline beneath brushed softly against my desk and printer's cabinet.

"Mister Ives," she said, but I held the palm of my hand up, flat and facing her.

"Stop. You promised you would call me John."

"I did. I'm sorry." A composer stick lay before her, half filled with cast iron letters. She put her index finger on some of them and traces of the thick ink smudged across her skin. "Why is this German?"

"We share our machines with the *Freie Presse* boys. There are as many Prussians as Mexicans around town." I offered my handkerchief and watched her as she wiped her fingers. I had not seen her in weeks, and suddenly sitting before me she was like a vein of silver in my day.

"I've come to make a disappeared persons notice in your newspaper, John. We are still looking for my sister and I think this might help us."

"We?" I grunted curtly.

Stella jumped in surprise at my tone. "My family. Mister Olenbush believes Lucy remains in San Antonio and my father would like to pursue that." She lay her book of notations between us, utterly unaware of my drowning love. "I'm sorry," she said. "Should I speak to someone else?"

"Of course not. I will be your agent here at the *Light*."

She nodded and slid the book to me. "In here is all I know of her now. I wrote down every detail Mister Olenbush told me."

I put my fingers on the leather binding but did not open it. "If she is anywhere in Bexar, we can ask that she contact you through this office. Is that what you prefer?"

I began to draft the announcement and when I finished, I read it aloud.

"Looking for Lucy Moore. Please contact John Ives at the *Light* offices— Would you like me to add that it's urgent she get in touch with you?"

"It's long been urgent, John," she replied and quickly wiped her cheeks of sudden tears. "My mother has not been well since Lucy ran."

Embarrassed and overcome, I looked down at the paper without speaking. I could hear her faltered breathing, but I was not trained in emotions or courage. "I could also do some searching farther out if you want."

"I couldn't pay you. I don't have anything more."

"Stella, I would never take money from you."

An interminable pause, a gulf, grew between us until she blurted, "It was on San Saba Street that Mister Olenbush saw her!"

"Where on San Saba?"

She held her back taut and her head high. "I'm sure you can imagine," she replied slowly, faltering. "A crib girl."

"And you are certain Olenbush is saying the truth?"

"Why wouldn't he be? He carried her photograph to compare."

Suddenly, the door opened, the wood panels slamming loudly closed with the arrival of my publisher. The hot breeze off the street shook the broadsheet pages that I had hung to dry on a line across the office. The sun through the window now cast a shadow over Stella's face and shoulders, balancing the light and the dark along the curves.

"Thank you." I stood, quickly shuffling my desk into order. "I'll be off then," I said to my boss, "if you've no more need of me. Miss Moore, may I accompany you home?"

The late sky was tawny with dust and sun. The two of us stepped past straw and trough of Commerce Street as we headed beyond the plaza toward the bridge. Breezes rising off the sour, summer river brought us the ripe smell of muck, and Stella steered us toward a tidy cottage to the south near the old Valero mission. I took her hand and nodded to her.

"Thank you," she said.

"I will read your notes tonight, and then we should fix an appointment to meet again."

"Of course."

A bricklayer worked the wall beside her cottage, mortaring and settling the pieces with a trowel he held like a weapon. She glanced at him and said, "So much here is new. Do we have a hope of finding her?"

"We can but try, Stella. And I understand a new copper was appointed to our ward last January. If you like, I will speak with him about our hunt."

"Oh, yes," she whispered. "Please. Mister Olenbush has refused to work with him; I think a grave mistake."

CHAPTER 5

olice and reporters have been known to drink at the same bars, and so I was not surprised that the very next noontime at the Silver King I saw that constable. He did not acknowledge me when I stood beside him, but bowed his head over a whiskey tumbler, his eyes glancing slowly from side to side under the narrow brim of his new bobby helmet.

I leaned across the counter and waved to Didier. "Beer, and another whiskey for our fine copper here."

The policeman turned to me staring. His eyes were small and dark, his skin dry and the color of ruddy dirt. He presented as a man of indeterminate age, and I suspected he might never have been at the heart of a child's game.

"My name is John Ives," I said and held out my hand.

"I'm Tom Broc." His voice was choppy and hoarse like a crow's, and he still wore his thick police jacket, sweating out through the wool. A nickel badge was pinned to his left breast pocket.

He took the tumbler, lifting his chin high to let the tobacco-laced whiskey slip down his throat. That is when I saw it, the permanent tattoo on his left cheek. Like black river worms coiling around each other, this crude drawing of two concentric circles held a four-pointed star inside them.

Broc watched my unabashed, childish stare. "That was long ago," he said at last. "I was taken as a slave outta New Orleans, brought over ta Baton Rouge by an Irishman who gave me to his Coushatta wife. They held me down one night and did this." He put a soiled fingernail to the circles. "Long time past. Means nothing now."

"I'm sorry," I said awkwardly.

He wore a thick, red cotton shirt, and began rolling the sleeves back over his elbows. "Been in San Antonio long?"

"Long enough to call it home."

Didier brought a crock of sour-smelling stew, placing it and a chunk of rye bread before him.

"Where's your birth home?" Tom asked me.

"Boston. At least, that's what I tell people."

"You don't speak the truth to folks, then?" He put the wide spoon to his lips and slurped the broth.

I smiled at his slyness. "Near enough, man. Do you tell all to all?" The unbroken rumble of carts hissed along the road outside. "In fact, I hail from Salem Village, from a long line of witches who were hanged by their neighbors."

He turned toward me raising his eyebrows, and I nodded. "Every grave holds a reason, but these days my family has turned from sorcery to mainline Episcopalian. As my father likes to remind me, we are the religion of presidents and successful men of industry."

"Sounds a man of keen insight, your father." Broc removed his jacket and settled back on his stool. "Must be good to have a pa looking out for you. As for me, I came with my family out the Swiss Jura but all of 'em ended up buried at the bottom of the Atlantic Ocean. Cholera. Shipmaster dumped me at the port in New Orleans when I was eleven. Learned to fish so as not to go hungry. I learned young not to expect kindness from people. A useful lesson." He took a chunk of bread and sopped up the grease from his bowl.

"I heard a rumor you worked the docks previously," I said. "True?"

Smirking, he asked, "True? Now what is truth to a fellow like you?" That quick fisherman's eye of his scouted me until at last he replied, "Yah, it's true. I was hired down to Galveston to look into the blackamoor dock jimmies haggling their wages."

"A rough profession, breaking up those associations."

"What makes you think I was a strikebreaker?"

"Anytime your sort ends up in the middle of such a storm, that'd be the job."

"Raise a lamp to my sort, then, boy," he said. "Longshoremen'd sooner kill you first and get to know you after."

"I'm not doubting that your line of work requires pluck, but I imagine the same is true of those dockers with hungry families. The only ones who profit are men like my father who invest in the shipping and the rails, although even he has borne a few troubles this year."

He watched the pitch of sunlight across the green felt of the gaming tables. Suddenly he said, "Everything is dangerous, my friend. Or nothing is, since we all find the same end."

Ayla Trinka came from the back room then, shuffling toward our voices and toeing the planked floor for obstacles. I held my hand out to bring her alongside us.

"Do you know Copper Broc? He comes from the Swiss mountains."

"I do," she said, looking slightly past him. "You been here a year yet, Tom?"

He leaned back and sighed. "No, only half, but we're a

growing town with opportunities for a peace officer. What brought you here, Miss Trinka?"

Ayla stared straight at his eyes like into a dark target. "I limped through these doors last year. Starved since the New Mexico Territories, and cold. Lost a tooth. Skin of my ankle burned away. My hip had popped sideways from a fall and Didier paid the doc to wrap me. Then I found the piano and he asked me to stay. You might say I was lucky both ways."

The old barman had been watching her, now ladling a bowl of soup and putting it in her hands. He came round the bar and stood beside her, leaning as he touched his lips to her cheek. With nothing broken or unfinished between them, Ayla took the spoon he offered and smiled, while Tom Broc looked on as though he didn't understand any of it.

"I'll be heading back to the *Light*, before they start counting the minutes I've been gone. But I would like to discuss a matter with you," I said. "When convenient. A missing persons matter."

"I'll come along now." He tossed his cigar to the floor, turning his heel into the boards as the deep, sweet smell rose around us. "Who do you seek?" he asked. He pushed into the street, his jacket under his arm, and bowed under the pecan branches overhanging the road.

"A runaway girl. The sister of a local teacher."

"Child?" His eyes were unaffected, utterly without reaction.

The road lifted in a gradual slope, and I stumbled over a rock rising from the hardpacked dirt. "Not at all." I took a deep breath. "Her grown sister. An investigator in town believes he saw the woman in the cribs on San Saba Street last spring."

"Name?"

"Lucy Moore, although I believe she also had a married name."

He stared as though dealing with a man lacking sense, and for a moment jammed his finger joints tight into fists. "Whores come 'n' go from this town," he said, his voice so strong that citizens passing us turned to watch. "Lots of 'em sick. Some just leave. Why, last spring one walked out into the blacklands and laid down dead. When we lifted her up, she shrieked like a mandrake stem even though the doc had declared her long passed."

"Nonetheless, I am seeking this Lucy Moore and would ask you to help."

To and fro with a curious eye, he watched me. "More details or a drawing would help, but I'll scout San Saba for you." He raised his spidery hands to stop me from speaking. "Who was investigating before?"

"Peter Olenbush, a teamster here in town."

"Olenbush?" he asked loudly. "I heard his name my first day. A German maybe on the run from the Missouri sheriffs. Story is he killed a couple in Saint Charles without motive. And it's said he once jumped in the Colorado River from a rail car as the train tore over the bridge near Yuma. The stoker saw him drop to the water in a shower of soot flakes. A wild man."

The fist of my heart was beating hard as I thought of Stella and Olenbush together. Meekly, I asked, "You believe all that?"

"I believe everything until I don't," he said.

"I know him a little," I said quietly. "These rumors seem bullied out of proportion. More truth of the teller than the told."

Shrugging, he said casually, "At the tables tonight?"

I nodded.

Abruptly, he asked, "What's the lost girl to you?"

"Her sister's an acquaintance."

"Kin of a whore?" he asked. "You oughta keep better comp'ny, Ives," but when I turned to answer he had already walked on.

Copper Tom Broc and I often met round the jackpots of an evening, for he had skill with brag and faro, and the complicated system called *tarocco*. Unlike anything else played in town, with an unrecognizable deck of cards that looked more like Romany sorcery than gambling, it took me weeks to learn its bent logic. But while nothing except my father's fortune ever came easily to me, I have always had tenacity. Eventually I learned the card pictures and the game, and as partners we clocked the tables clean, often ending our evenings so late and so successfully we had no care for where we put our heads. One dawn after such a night, we found ourselves on the platform of the International & Great Northern station, sleeping sole to sole on benches while the breaking light fanned out across us.

"Not good, John Ives, not good," he said, pulling himself upright.

I lifted my hat from my eyes, brushing the dust from the stiff tweed waistcoat covering my chest. "Unbecoming for the local law? Or a Pinkerton strikebreaker?"

"That's a career I would not return to. Dock jimmies're the lowest types." He shook his head. "What's it like to grow up in a mansion on Beacon Hill?"

I sat straight up into the loud, already unbearable sun. "Depends on whether your windows overlook the south slope or the north, my friend. And how do you know where my home is?"

"You told me Boston, didn't you?" He pulled a roll of bills from his front pocket, fanning them at me. "And you already know I'm clever."

On the far side of the rails stood a lone cow, her head too heavy for her sloped neck, and a calf fixed hard to her udder. Two olive-skinned women on mules plodded from the alley behind the station house, slipping down from their mounts and positioning themselves near us to wait for the early train.

"San Antonio seems a long way from the temples of the city for a fellow like you," I said.

"Boss in Galveston dug this grave for me." He watched the awkward mule women tug hard at their animals. "Offered me a small job with a big price, and when that was done, found me the copper work." He reached down to tear off a wayside bloom of wild bluebonnets. "What's not to desire? Big hungry girls with naught better to do than serve. A bundle of easy winnings."

The first streetcar had not yet departed the stable barn, so we set off walking crosstown back to the Silver King. Though the morning heat suffocated, Tom wore his wool jacket, wrinkled now from our serious tomfoolery with the tables and the women and the sweaty sleep. Frequently he took his gloves from his breast pocket and brushed them down across his coat and trousers, as though stains or dirt or the memory of the night could be dashed away by doing so.

When we reached our destination I said, "I'll stand you to breakfast, Tom." I touched his shoulder and he jerked back as though a shiver of electricity railed through him.

"Why?" he asked, not smiling.

"Just my thanks for a fine night of leisure." I turned to the door and hammered on it with my fist until the latch slipped.

"Yah yah!" called a woman from the inside, and when the outer oak swung wide, Ayla stood on the threshold. "Eager you all are today. Starving, is it?"

"It's just us, Ayla," I said. "Your two favorite suitors."

She smiled and closed her eyes against the harsh light. "John and Olenbush," she said confidently, "I'll fetch you some coffee," and the moment Tom heard the other's name, he frowned silently and pushed past her into the dining room.

CHAPTER 6

On a Saturday afternoon at the end of a sweaty week, I cleaned and locked our office only to find Tom Broc in the road with a runaway goat that had come to drink from a nearby trough.

"What you doing there, officer?" I called. "Not enough crime in your section today?"

His fingers held fiercely to the base of the animal's horns. "Rounding up lost livestock," he replied, "and maybe gambling men such as yourself wanting a meal and a game."

"I'm in with you tonight. Been a long and tedious day."

"Is it the Silver King or the White Elephant? Or maybe somewhere new?" He heaved hard at the goat, pushing it back to the water and releasing it. Turning to me, his blue eyes pale and hard as diamonds, he said, "Or we could go down San Saba for a lookie-loo." Without waiting for my answer, he set off striding heel first with the confidence of the unbridled law. He turned away from Commerce Street and I followed, while behind us the flange of the last train squealed as it made the turn into town.

San Saba was filled with souls clamoring on corners, cheap crib girls waiting before their doors, and ravenous men dodging into doorways at the sight of our copper. The closer we advanced, the slower he strolled until we reached Nueva Street on the far side of the creek, where he halted abruptly.

"We'll stop at the Cortez place," he said. "Ask a few questions." We paused to let a cart pass the corner, and Broc looked hard at me. "Pull that cabinet card out, there. Let me see it again."

I slipped it from my jacket pocket and handed it over. "The one in the middle is our lost woman," I said.

"And which is Stella Moore?"

I stared at him for I had not yet disclosed the name of the girl who tied me to San Antonio. "You are one damnably excellent detective," I said.

He held the photograph in his fist and spirited himself quickly across the road toward a grizzle-haired woman standing on the porch of an oddly ornate two-story building. When I landed at his heels the two were conversing in a Spanish I did not recognize, filled with guttural grunts reminiscent of the Huastecs I knew in the highlands above Tampico. The woman buzzed like a ruffled warbler, laughing with Tom in that golden late afternoon light, and though her jowls were creased and her back humped high like a hog's, the molten pulse of her sweet black eyes brought me close to ruin.

Missus Cortez waved us through the silken curtains at the door and into her parlor. Of course I had been to the cheap cribs, but short of dollar as I was, never to such elegance as the world of Ignacia Cortez. Beyond the cool, blue silk drapes was a parlor to rival my mother's in its taste. Spreading before us lay a thick, loomed carpet in silver and deep blue; fine, French glass lamps the color of soft alabaster flickered on carved tables while men and women with glasses of champagne relaxed on satin-covered armchairs.

"Take your time and enjoy yourselves," she said to us. A

thick, gold necklace lay at her throat and she touched it now with chubby fingers. "Ask the ladies about your girl, and when you're ready they will show you in to the gaming."

Tom Broc nodded, and Missus Cortez left us.

"This is as fine as any literary salon in Boston," I whispered.

"You really are a poor winter boy, aren't ya?" he replied. "Don't know what you're seeing when ya see it, even." He said it like a cock, bobbing and pecking.

"Oh, I do. I've seen more of the world than you think, Broc. Been down in Mexico where the whores can and do kill their prey."

He didn't respond, and in the pause we heard shouts of distant men raging under the dying light of day, followed by the echo of a single gunshot.

"You may have more urgent responsibilities than our search for Lucy Moore," I said, but he only shrugged.

A woman came to us then, skin white as milk and delicate pink lace covering her breasts. I saw her throw a glance at Tom, but he plunged into the room following a different girl, his hat under his arm, his damp hair clinging to his skull, and the black curls of his tattoo glossed by the light.

"What d'ya want to drink?" she asked me. "Champagne?"

"Most fine," I replied.

She put her hand across mine. "Come, then," she said, and led me to a broad green velvet bench where I sat until she returned with my drink.

"What is your name?" I asked, and her bare shoulder caught the light like porcelain. Brazenly, I put my fingertips on the hollow beside her collarbone.

"Mary," she said at last.

"Your real given name?"

"Of course," she said, guffawing so loudly I knew I would never know her true name.

"Well, Mary, I'm here to find a disappeared girl. Name of Lucy Moore. Ever heard of her?"

"What's her specialty?"

"I understand that she was once married to a preacher, and sometimes preaches herself."

Mary began to laugh again. "Praising Gabriel is not often considered a specialty at Cortez's house." She swept her hands down her bodice, smoothing the pink lace. "Are you here for me or for this girl?"

"For the girl. Yellow hair and green eyes, round face, thin mouth. Here," I said, and pulled out the photograph. "Plain girl. Seen her?"

"I been in Bexar three years and seen a dozen girls of that type in the parlors. No one here like that now, though."

Before I could press further, I heard the street door open. The blue curtains parted, and standing in the doorway was Olenbush, red-faced and leaning hard on the jamb.

Glaring through the cigar smoke directly at me, he laughed and called out, "Been looking for you all night! Well, I dig no more, Johnny." In his right hand dangled a pocket pistol and he walked unsteadily toward me.

I had the time to dash away, but instead I stood tall and held my arms out to him.

The craters of his eyes were on fire, and a stride away from my outstretched hands he stumbled, chuckling as he hit the carpet. I rushed to help him stand, gripped his shoulders and hefted him up, but he looked at me with drooping eyelids and slumped to his knees. He lay wheezing, his clothes soaked in the smell of brandy.

"I've been shot," he whispered.

"Where? What did you do?" I asked.

"Only what you would've." Then so quietly I scarcely heard

him, "Damn farmers beating on a little 'un. I had 'em, though. They'll think before they go after a child again."

From the far corner of the parlor, I heard the Cortez woman say, "Get that gun from his hand," and I reached for the Colt, but a larger, stronger hand pulled at it first.

Above me stood a bearded Lucifer, heavy at the gut and tall.

Cortez said to her guard, "Get him out, Santiago, and bring me the gun. I've had enough of Olenbush for a lifetime."

"I'll help him home," I offered. "He's a friend of mine."

Santiago leaned forward and grabbed Olenbush at his armpits, dragging him toward the door, but as the body moved it left a wake of deep red, thick as blood sap across the blue and silver threads.

"He's bleeding!" I shouted. "Roll him over to see."

Others in the room gathered round but the guard did not quit.

"Go get that copper," Cortez said to one of her women. "Santiago, check to see if life is in him still."

The goliath stopped pulling at Olenbush and turned him, smashing his face to the carpet. I knelt beside my friend and whispered, "Where is your wound, Peter?" He lifted his head to tell me, but didn't speak.

"He lives, then," said Ignacia Cortez.

"Here, John," said Tom, standing now beside me on the blood-soaked carpet. "We'll get him to Doc Hunnicutt's place. You," he said to Santiago, "bring the wagon round to the door."

We carried Olenbush into the twilit road, a dim, gray moon stamped against the horizon. We laid him in the box of the cart and I sat beside him, my jacket under his head as we bounced upon the road. Once past the irrigation canal and its seedy trees, we turned into the noise and lantern light of the plaza. Before us crushed a dozen men or more, angrily lurching at each other, grunting and falling with the crack of breaking bones and gunshots.

Holding hard at the reins, Tom shouted, "I leave you here! Come quick and take these! There's work for me."

I scrambled to the bench, grabbing the reins while Broc leaped to the ground with his Colt in the air. He fired several times at the sky, but it did nothing to calm the chaos.

"He won't last the night," Tom said over his shoulder, and turning, ran like a hellhound into the brawl.

Beside me on the bench sat the cart lantern, and I lifted it high over Peter's face. He lay with open eyes and even breath, his lips forming a monkey's smile.

CHAPTER 7

The next day, I sat behind my desk in the Commerce Street office, stiff and disinterested, my knuckles knocking out seconds that were rendered interminable by the two young men in front of me.

"This town'll claim a victim most weeks," drawled the first. "Yesterday musta' brought down a dozen, though the scramble was quick finished." They described the mob of the previous night in the most belabored detail, and now lingered in my office adding their opinions.

The second said, "Depends on the weather, and if they get hold of sommit. Shoulda' seen Olenbush. That Deutschy were like a javelina pig swallowin' strychnine." Although they both wore clean shirts no doubt ironed by their doting mothers, the smell of cow muck rose around us from the unpolished leather of their work shoes. "We was havin' fun is all. Weren't gonna kill that nigger boy."

"Thank you, fellas," I said, standing behind the desk. "Spell your names for me now, please, in the event I need to quote you."

The first one shook his head. "I can write mine. Gimme that

pencil." He grabbed it and began his name on the top blue line of my paper, pressing so hard as to cause ridges in the desktop beneath. "The scramble only lasted minutes," he muttered in a voice oddly deep for a farmboy. "How many unlucky dead this mornin'?" he asked, looking up at me of a sudden with a broody stare. His left eyelid was purpled and swollen, his cheeks bruised from last night's punches.

"Four," I replied, "although after the first death, there really is no other, is there?"

He looked at me puzzled, then put a rough hand to his crotch and scratched from side to side, and as he did, he loosened the oily odor of days of unwashed toil.

"Counting the Deutschy?" his colleague asked.

"No. Doctor Hunnicutt says he is still among us."

"That be cruel, then," the first said. "Four good men died from his knife and gun, all for the sake a' one little nigra boy."

I walked to the door to wave them gone but could not resist muttering, "How do you know they were good men?"

His eyes widened. "They was folks like us. Worked hard for what they got."

I held the door open and when they had stomped away, I set about to write the news of their dead colleagues and my friend.

By lunchtime, I put my pencil in its tray and sat quietly in a slant of hot light cutting through the broad streetside pane. The dust glimmered across the floor, sharp and sparkling, while this torn town rumbled outside. Overwhelmed by the dust and the heat and the fishy stink of linseed oil, I grabbed my hat and pistol, locked the door, and turned toward Hunnicutt's surgery. Nearing Soledad and surrounded by a clean, cloudless sky and deep old trees hanging heavy with summer apples, I saw a child in the turning, hiding in the alley beside the surgery.

"Rufus Sams?" I was near enough to see his tears.

He nodded. "Yessir."

"Were you in that fight last night?"

Tentatively, he took a child's step back and said, "Yeah. I brung it on."

"You here to see Peter Olenbush?"

"Yessir."

"Come then, I'll take you in."

"I be trouble if ya do."

"Ridiculous. Come." I took his small, calloused hand and climbed the step to the door. As I did, the boy squirmed free and ran. Like a fool beholding the grail, I shook my head in judgment.

Doctor Hunnicutt opened that door even before I could knock, and he stood by my side watching the back of Rufus Sams escape into the alley.

"So many of these ragamuffins," he said. "What good did it do to preserve the country and kill our thousands? Now these pickaninnies run the streets, where before they at least learned skills on the farms."

I closed my gaping mouth. I knew of his allegiance to the Knights of the Golden Circle, but as a green reporter, my success in this town rested on my relationships with civic leaders such as Hunnicutt. I stood silently for a moment, watching a hackney driver trundle his human cargo past. A turkey vulture landed on the empty lot across, kissing the dust with its white beak, and my agitation spilled.

"He does have a home, though," I blurted. "Lives over in Ellis Alley. Has a brother and a mother. He only came here like me, to see his friend."

Hunnicutt raised both eyebrows, and I could tell his vanity was burning. "How do you know all of that, sir?" He had come out through the door suddenly, holding a dinner napkin between his fingers, and his yellow teeth still gnawing at a morsel of gristle.

"I work at the *Light*. It's my business to keep abreast."

"You desire to see Mister Olenbush?"

"He lives still?"

"Of course. Much worse for his irresponsible deeds, but I cleaned him and pulled the bullet from his back. He bled a bucket, though. Come in, Mister Ives."

The windowless surgery was a nightmarish combination of bodily rubbish and the sweet smell of chloroform.

"How do you operate without light?" I asked.

"By lantern is always best." He stood before long shelves of bottles of all sizes, marked in a shaking hand with the names of roots and liquids, black bottles of chloroform, calomel, quinine, and an entire shelf of ether. He was a small man, and hunched slightly forward from the waist. Rolling down each sleeve, he fastened his links to the cuffs. "Olenbush is in the far room. I'll leave you to it."

My friend sat propped in a deep chair, surrounded by delicate antimacassar cloths over the back and arms of the upholstery. A dead clock stood behind him, and what windows there were in the small recovery room had been shuttered. A wick lamp burned down on the small table beside him, casting thin light in an otherwise bright afternoon.

Pillows held his shoulders straight, but his head lolled to one side.

"Peter," I said, and walked to him. "Thank God."

He lifted his head and shrugged. "I live, Johnny. And live to do it again." He opened his green eyes wide.

"You had more luck than you can imagine," I said.

"Will you take me home, Johnny? I'm seeing and hearing things never brought on by whiskey."

"If Hunnicutt will allow it."

He stood wearily and shook his head. "His is a rogue's

judgment, friend. I'll go on my own, then." He took a step, paused, and took another.

"Doctor told me you lost blood. You'll be too weak to leave on your own," I said.

"I'll do it." He smiled and added, "I can see the hay fields from here. Soft hay, and smelling like wine." He took another step, and I grabbed his elbow. "The doc is a serpent," he said. "Believe that."

As he would not stop for me, I followed him through the house while Hunnicutt sat at a table among his potions, watching us.

"I'll need a cart to take me home. Think I just took all my steps for now."

"He won't make it to the end of Soledad!" the doctor called out to us, but Peter pressed on, and once in the afternoon daylight, leaned exhausted against the doorpost.

I raised my arm and skedaddled into the road, bringing the next empty hack to halt before Hunnicutt's porch. The wind had lifted hard, and as I helped him into the rig, Peter lurched forward in the gusts.

"The Sisters' infirmary should be your destination. Not your own rooms."

"I'd drown in the river before choosing the church." He chuckled faintly as the driver and I hoisted him onto the hard bench. Climbing in, I grabbed his shoulders and held him steady. "Not a word to Stella," he whispered, and his eyes were wicked with ardor.

"Why not? She's an excellent nurse."

"Not one word," he muttered. "I don't need her pity."

The hackman drove into the far west of town, to a clutch of sultry roads worked by hungry, angry families of freedmen. We were yet a street away from his rooms when our cabber pulled his mare up and said this, "I'll need a higher price to deliver any closer."

I shook my head at the man's greed, even as he carried a dying soul on his bench. "And what price would that be?" I asked.

"I'll be pleased to doorstep ya' for a clean dollar," he said, "Silver, of course." He flashed a broad gob grin that quickly faded into a frown.

I gulped. "So be it," I said and reached into my pocket. "Move on, man. My friend needs water."

He snapped the whip and down we went, farther still into the bowels of town, fast as we could to keep the flint of Olenbush alive.

Once he lay abed, I remained beside him, standing in a brittle husk of light. He sighed and groaned, then fell to sleep but I did not leave for he had pulled a fever that wouldn't break. His landlady covered him with woolen blankets and he remained a woebegone smoldering pile.

A hard knock came at the door. Through the crack I saw the copper eyes of Rufus Sams.

"Come in," I said, swinging the door wide. Behind him stood a tall Mexican woman, her hair and face draped with a blue lace mantilla. When she stepped into Peter's room she bowed her head slightly beneath the jamb. She smelled of tarragon; indeed, she carried a basket over one arm and clutched fresh tarragon leaves, still bearing their golden flowers.

The boy stepped forward. "This is my mama. She came to help."

I looked at the woman and back to Rufus. "What should I call you, Señora?"

"Call her nothing," said a second boy, his brother, Jaime, who stood behind Rufus, the same copper eyes but dark, African skin. "She is *curandera*, a healer. You don't need her name." He could not have been more than thirteen years, but he spoke with authority, hovering beside the woman they both called mother.

She rolled the tarragon between her palms, crushing it again and again until the sweet scent of pine and licorice covered us all. She pulled Peter's sheets down to his waist, spreading open his muslin sleepshirt. Spitting in her hands, she rolled the tarragon once more between her fingers, then spread the poultice across his chest, smoothing and rubbing it into his skin.

"*Lo tiene que voltear.*" She gestured to show she wanted him turned over, then unfolded a cloth from the basket. She knelt beside it on the floor, pulling strips of brittle, gray bark from it. Her older son handed her a pot and mallet, and Señora Sams began to grind.

Not sure how to roll an injured man without hurting him, I watched her without moving, anxiously remembering Huasteco *curanderos* operating in the Tampico jungles. All of them had lost patients before my eyes.

"Turn him!" she exclaimed. The boys and I stepped to the bed and obeyed.

She lifted the long linen bandage and batting from my friend's body, and moved her head in disgust as the smell of bromine overcame us. Rufus reached into the basket and handed his mother a thick branch of cactus. She peeled the skin and needles from it and cleaned Peter's wound with the moist cactus flesh, stroking hard and slow over his back until the doc's oily brown antiseptic stains had disappeared from the torn red skin where the bullet had entered.

She looked at Rufus. "Bring me mud from the river now," and when he returned she molded a shell over the invalid's back and the bloody hole. As Olenbush slept, she pulled me aside. "Will you be his keeper?"

"Me? No. Well, at times, but not always. I have responsibilities."

"He needs a nurse. And that nurse must rub these powders into the soles of his feet. Two times each day." She handed me the pot of pulverized bark. "Don't forget." She wrapped her neck and shoulders in the blue lace, packed her basket, and nodded at her children. "Come," she said to them.

I peered between the curtains as Señora Sams and her boys walked into the hot, starry night. That was when I noticed Tom Broc standing in a cone of moonlight, staring from me to the Sams family, and back.

CHAPTER 8

The *curandera* instructed Rufus to care for Peter rather than attend school, and so he did, toting water, bringing him food, and applying powders and muslin wrapping to his protector's body. I managed to visit our wounded friend only occasionally, of a dinnertime or sly minutes I stole from investigations on behalf of my publisher.

Midweek I found Peter alone, sitting upright in bed. Naked to the waist but for the bandages, reeking of tarragon and the liquor that he drank freely, the man was clearly too stubborn to die.

"Where's the boy?" I asked.

"Didn't come today."

I cocked one eyebrow. "Sure you didn't send him off?" I asked, watching him closely. "I'll stay with you then."

"No need. My mama always told me I never cried at pain."

"You are still close to dying, Peter." I opened the window to cleanse the air in the room.

"No, shut it. The street noise keeps me from sleep."

I did not, but walked to him and asked, "Have you changed

your bandages this morning?" I reached out to touch the wrap, but he pushed my hand away.

"Just sit with me. I don't need a nurse."

"You do, man. Your face looks gray as a rotting gourd."

He smiled weakly, and through the open window came the sound of the horse-drawn trolley and the obstinate shouts of workers. "Soon as they built the first rail line in, townspeople went mad. Now I hear they're aiming the tracks to California and down to Mexico," he said.

"A long, slow effort," I replied, and sat in the window chair by the fresh, warm air. "My father put some money in it. Convinced his friends as well. Ran out of track and cash, though, before they got very far, and his investors weren't happy about that. He's been fighting off lawyers ever since."

He yawned broadly and as he did, closed his eyes like an unchristened child.

"Why did you leave home for Texas, Peter?" I asked, my childish wish desiring a story of a killing or thieving or some lost Missouri girl growing his baby in her belly.

"Brother'n me rode south one day getting clear of family rot. Left our little sister behind in St. Charles."

"You're an orphan?"

"No, but some lives're worse than what you find in orphanages."

I could barely hear his words above the road noise and the pottering of steps on the stairs, but his face returned my own grief.

"Whatever happened to that brother of yours?" I asked.

"He's up in Falls County. Railroader. Quiet fellow." He paused. "You wanna be this side of the truth, John? I'll tell ya, he's got a life I wouldn't take. Five children and a wife, daybreak job he'll never escape."

"And your sister?"

"She didn't make it out of St. Charles alive." And before he moved again beneath the linen, he said this, "Our house was a dark place. We never shoulda left her to fend. Men like our father don't belong on this earth. Leaving her behind like we did, well that's the meaning of sin. Never again."

Just then the slanted door to his room pushed open, and in the shaft of hallway light stood Rufus, accompanied by Stella.

"Miss pressed me to bring 'er!" the child said.

"Yes, I did," Stella added. "No student avoids my classroom without permission, and certainly not three days in a row. I've come to assess your situation, Mister Olenbush."

Desperate, the boy stared at Peter. "I'm sorry!"

Smiling a crooked smile, he reached his hand out. "Come here, Rufe."

"Stella," I said, "please wait outside and give our friend a moment to clothe himself."

"I've tended male patients before. You, for example." She stood straight as an elm, but the heat of Peter's cheeks overcame her, and she slipped to the other side of the door.

"Bloody hell's flames," he hissed, teetering from the bed to set his drink on the cupboard. "Get me my clothes, boy."

He pulled a work shirt over his head, grimacing with the stretch of his bandaged back. He sat hard in a chair by the window and held his side until his face relaxed. Raking his fingers through his hair, he set his jaw and stood to adjust his trousers. He took a small bottle of Köln water from the washstand beside him and put it to his lips, rinsing and spitting, and returning to lower himself into a chair.

"Now," he said, and Rufus opened the door.

"Mister Olenbush," Stella commenced even before she was entirely in the room, "you cannot keep a child from his lessons." She pushed the door wide behind her and crossed to the bureau where an empty whiskey bottle lay. Wrapping her fingers around its neck, she lifted it high, shaking her head.

"You used to call me Peter."

"You are changing our topic. I am discussing Rufus Sams and his education. You can't avoid my point by ignoring it." A hairpin had slipped her curls and dangled beside her temple. I desperately desired to re-pin it, or pull the others free, or perhaps merely touch the lone lock that fell upon her face.

"The boy is only obeying his mother, the *curandera*," I explained, while Olenbush stared at Stella like a sulky tom. "Not a request from Peter at all."

"Is that true?" She waited, pulling the curl from her face and looping it behind her ear. "All I heard was that you had been in the town fight. No one mentioned injuries." She moved closer to his chair, allowing the palm of her hand to hover over his own. "Your lips are blue. What's happened?"

With a skill that rivaled a naughty child's, Peter bent his head forward while at the same time opening his green eyes wide. Glancing up at her, he whispered, "I haven't been well, Stella."

"Please sit with us," I said. "Peter may need more help than he is willing to accept."

She took the chair opposite him. "Are you wounded?" Around her neck stood starched white cotton folded to scallops just below her jawline. She wore a simple gray dress of thick wool, cinched at her small waist and slightly belled to the floor. The color of the dress was the same as her eyes, pale as nacre shell.

"A bullet to my side," he replied.

"Have you seen the doctor?"

"Yah, but he's a charlatan, my dear. Devoted to hate more than healing." Peter shifted uncomfortably on his chair, and grimaced again, inhaling sharply. "Wouldn't even let poor Rufus in to see me."

Stella lurched forward. "Is Rufus the only one who has been tending to you?"

"What lovely attire you wear for those lucky children, Stella," he muttered.

"The *curandera* brought bark powder and bathed him. She's very skilled in her own way," I said.

Stella looked slowly from Peter to me and back again. "Has Doctor Hunnicutt seen you since?"

"That man doesn't treat people down this part of town," I said.

"Well, the Sisters, then?"

We looked at her without answering.

"God gave both of you five senses but no brains," she said. "I'm leaving now but I'll be back this afternoon with treatments. Rufus, come with me."

"Thank you, Stella," Peter said, straining forward in the chair, closer to her. He put his hand out to touch hers, but she did not return the grasp. "Ah, Johnny, would you fetch me water, friend? A huge thirst has come over."

I turned to the pitcher and poured, grumbling, "Doc Hunnicutt saved your life that night, Peter. Don't forget that. Whatever you think of his philosophies, he mended you when the need arose."

I heard him grunt in response, but when I turned round with his water, his fingers were grasping the collar of Stella's dress, his lips pressed against hers, his tongue seeking taste while leaving sheen across her skin.

Despondent, I watched and heard the echo of a single tone rise from somewhere, a surly B-flat note, until I realized this to be my own groan.

Stella put both hands firmly against Peter's chest and pushed him down into the chair. "Never do that again. There is no excuse for such bad behavior." She grabbed Rufus's hand and pulled him into the hall. "Make sure you are presentable when I return." The fresh, light scent of ginger root remained in the room after her.

"How can you take advantage of the girl's kindness?" I asked. "You are the worst kind of thief, Peter."

He pitched himself forward to stand, grabbed a cotton pouch from the nightstand, and rolled the chopped tobacco into a small paper he held between his fingertips. He added a slight twist to each end and a quick lip-flick to stick them closed, then took a kitchen match from his shirt pocket. Edging back to the bed, he grabbed the whiskey tumbler and smiled. "Maybe. But her skin has a sweet taste to it, as I thought it would."

"Now that the child saw what you did, the whole town will hear, and Stella could be terminated as a teacher. Why would you take such liberties with her?"

"Stella's heart will come to me. You'll see."

"Because you thieved a kiss? Don't be ridiculous."

Tallow-eyed, he sat on the side of the bed. His face was stubbled and wan yet somehow still handsome, his soul entirely undeserving. "The summer'll die soon and you'll be back in Tampico, having understood nothing," he said, jutting his chin at me and narrowing his eyes. "Rufus'll not speak of that kiss. But perhaps you will, Johnny? Is that it? After all, your job is to publish what you see as long as any damned towners want to read the gossip."

"Keep a civil tongue, Olenbush. I've been an honorable friend."

He smiled again, his lips thin, his jaws clenched. "Honor among foxes, I think. Like father, like son."

"What? My father? You don't even know my father, just what you've read."

He lay back and pulled the yellowing coverlet across his

shoulders, exposing bloodstains on the linen. "I'll sleep now. No need for you to stay."

I didn't move for the door. "What you want from her will ruin her," I said.

With a face as dry as a ghost's and pale, too, he put his cigarette to his lips and sucked hard, the yellow of his fingernails pressing to white. "You and I want the same, but I'll be honest where you will scheme."

A chair sat between him and me, and I kicked it toward the window. "Were you truthful when you took Stella's money to find her sister and reported that you saw the girl in the cribs? I read through her notebook filled with your reports. I've been down Nava and San Saba. Not a single person recognizes the image of Lucy Moore. You were preying on Stella from the day you first met."

"Was I?" He lay his smoking quirly on a tray beside the bed and pushed himself to sit. "Such a false friend, you are." Swinging his legs over the side of the bed, he spun his fingers up through the smoke like a magician and planted his feet on the floor. "All your anger cannot beat me, even wounded as I am. Move on me now, or leave."

"I took you for a chum, Peter."

"And I have been."

"You know I love her, and I know you don't. A story old as water."

For a moment his stare was weary, nearly blind, and he did not reply. In the gut of that silence, I slipped from the room and didn't return.

CHAPTER 9

Two months later toward the end of September, the sun became less of an enemy, and I began to welcome its soft warmth over the city's horizon. On one such dawn, I walked down the plaza to meet Tom Broc at the Silver King, and there found Ayla Trinka sitting at a gaming table with dozens of rusty nails strewn before her. Taking them one by one in the palm of her hand, she stroked each and arranged it back on the green felt. I stood inside the batwing doors, while the dim morning light cut across her lips and cheeks and the nails.

"You alone, Miss Ayla?" I asked.

She held out her calloused hand. "You're early, John. Don't usually see you before dinnertime. Coffee or whiskey?" She lifted a tin mug from the corner shelf below the table and gulped from it.

Moving closer I took her hand, and her skin was rough as a cow's tongue. "Coffee," I said, "but I'll find Didier to fetch it. Stay where you are, my dear." I lifted one of the thick, wrought nails, the smell of dust rising. "What are you doing with these?"

"Sorting the useful from them needs retooling. They're graveyard nails arrived from Galveston this week. Didier and young Broc'r sending the good ones up the hill for new coffins." She continued stroking and sorting the twisted from the straight. "They see a decent price so Didier bought half the lot from Broc."

"Such big trade even out here at the edge of nowhere," I replied. "My father would be proud of this town."

"Your father?" Tom Broc stood at the doors, peering into the room. "What about your father?"

"Nothing," I said. "A joke is all."

"I heard rumor that you been cut off by your father."

Surprised by such a personal revelation of my embarrassment, I scowled at him saying, "I thought you police worked with facts not rumors."

"We work with all, boy." He poked into the piles of iron strewn across the table. "Heard a story about a rich son suddenly needing to fend. Matched it up with you and look now, you just confirmed it for me!" He paused to chuckle and muttered, "Well, I suppose your father was figurin' a way to drive you outta childhood."

He looked directly at me without mercy. Green as I was, exposed as I was, I had no response and only stared silently at him while Ayla nipped the rust off each nailpoint with her fingers. Finally, she asked Broc, "Why is Galveston sending old coffin nails to Bexar?"

"Hurricane wiped out their cemetery. Bones floated out to sea but left behind the iron and the lumber." From the kitchen annex rose the rich smell of boiling honey, sulfurous and sweet at once, and he lifted his chin to inhale. "Sir is trying out my method for honey mead, I think."

"Not too absorbed to make us some food, is he?" I asked Ayla. "Tom and I planned to take breakfast together."

She stood up, both hands flat on the table for balance. "I'll see to it. Johnnycake and pork good?"

"Anything you have will be sufficient," I said.

Tom slipped into her chair and took a fistful of the nails, calling to her back, "These turned out to be a good cargo."

I sat across from him. "It seems we both have connections with Galveston."

He arched an eyebrow. "Explain, please."

"My father put money into that port. To advance his Mexican interests."

"Lotsa men did and ended up on easy street," he said, his blue eyes narrowing. "Your father included. Never met him, but old Theophilus Ives showed his face a time or two on the docks." His mouth, mad with a smile, broadened and he added, "Bad luck for us detectives, though. We came outta there with only a cartful of coffin nails."

I inched my chair forward, close enough that he could hear a whisper. "Listen, Broc, I had a new thought about the disappeared girl." I pulled from my pocket the small scribblebook belonging to Stella. "I've been rereading Miss Moore's notes, and I think another truth might be clear in here."

"The teacher's thoughts?" he asked. "I read them before. Don't be coy, John. Tell me what you know."

The calls of men from the road rose, oxcarts grinding too, and the grating of the first streetcars of the day.

"I spent some time with Olenbush over the summer and found a side to his character I hadn't anticipated. Impetuous and not altogether honest."

He unbuttoned his waistcoat, leaned back, and with the clean voice of a bell, said, "I heard you both're desiring to court the teacher."

I stood up abruptly. "That's a rumor I wouldn't give any credence."

He waved his hand as though I were a child. "Oh, sit. And stop denying what can be observed. Just because you write about this town doesn't mean you can change the facts." He grabbed his cup of coffee grog and downed it, the dark slop splashing down his jaw. "I've known Olenbush for a good while and his honesty has never improved."

"You knew him before Bexar?"

"Of course. Pinks see these men again and again." He lifted a handful of nails, dusty and scabbed in rust.

"Have you ever had occasion to jail him?"

Broc's clawed, cold stare took me aback. "Once," he said. "And I'd be cheered to put him up for life."

"For what crime?

"It was a long time ago." He shrugged, his eyebrows raised. "Again, I'm asking. What new evidence have you uncovered about Miss Moore's sister? Those cheap whores go missing every day from the houses in San Antonio, and others come to take their place. Whether they die or run, we'll never know. I even hear some end up in variety shows."

"I don't think Olenbush ever met the sister. All he ever told Stella was what you and I could see from the cabinet card of the girls, what she looked like, her personality, all sewn up in what Stella herself had already told him. Seems to me he probably gave her bits of information for his own romantic interests."

"Why d'you think I'd care if he never met the sister? I don't believe it's a crime to tell a girl a lie to get her close to you."

"No, but it's a crime to take money under false promises, isn't it? I believe he took her for every penny she had, lied about San Saba, watched Stella grieve, all the while polishing his romantic opportunity."

Broc leaned back in the chair, his eyes in the shadows. "I think you're wrong," he said, "and I'm sure not wasting my police time on this fairy tale of your lost conquest." The sweet smell of mead turned to burning honey around us and he looked to the cookery door, smiling. "That's the error they all make. You have to watch that pot even when you can't take the boredom anymore."

"Wrong? You think Olenbush was acquainted with the sister?"

"I do," he said, and then naturally as bird trills rising in the day, he added, "In fact, I think he was the end of her."

My throat suddenly dry, I coughed, wheezed, and spoke again. "With what purpose?"

"Purpose? Men like that need no purpose. They murder from brass and dazzle as much as reason."

The smell of char from the kitchen overcame the sweet until I could no longer breathe evenly. "I was only speaking of seduction, Tom. Leading Stella on for romantic purposes. Murder is another realm."

"I'm a simple jack. In these lands, the meaning of disappearance is often death, and the meaning of death is normally slaughter." He took his bowler from his skull and set it atop the nails. "No one I've talked to has seen the girl since last winter, yet Olenbush says there's a witness who did. Maybe he's just dodging blame himself. Might have had conversations with her. Might even know where she's buried." He spread his fingers on his thighs and pushed himself to stand.

In his eyes I saw the last light of voices he might have heard as a child, resting deep in some wound. "I know you believe he was your friend and I'm sorry for that. But I suggest you choose more wisely next time." He laid it before me as a chapter ended, and his words, which often held the tang of venom, fell quietly. "And while you poke around for a reason why Miss Moore won't return your lusty affection, if you find any evidence of a crime, I'd happily investigate."

"What makes you believe she is dead?" I asked, thinking of my poor, sad Stella if that were true.

Didier strode into the room carrying our meals, cutting away the smell of the burned mead with that of greased pork. "I followed your instructions," he said smiling at Broc, "and now have a shambles to clean."

Broc sat again and ate in a silence so colossal I could not resist speaking. "But what proof do you have for this opinion of Olenbush?"

"Proof?" He shook his head and shrugged. "I can wait for proof."

CHAPTER 10

Broc was not to be found at the tables that evening or those following. Though coppers often swanned about in other wards of the city, his absence in ours began to gnaw by the new workaday week, so I sought him in the salons and the plazas, among the teamsters and chili queens and vaqueros. At last I spotted him down the far bend of the river in Soledad alley, standing between the Schmidt warehouse and the blue door of Doc Hunnicutt's surgery. Arms akimbo, fingers tight in fists, he bent forward in fury, facing a youth. Drawing closer, I recognized the boy to be Rufus's older brother, Jaime.

The west wind stoked the streets with dust and sound, and though I could not hear a word Broc shouted, his mouth was curled with madness. Thinking to save the trembling boy from such feral rage, I ran down the riverbank toward them, coming first to a stable of whinnying animals. In the broad doorway stood my publisher, tugging hopelessly at his mare.

"Ives!"

I looked to Broc and the boy and back to my employer. "Yessir?"

"Go inside and get the bucket." He spoke with clear eyes and a tinge of ice to his words.

I looked down Soledad again for Broc and the boy, but only saw their backs as our copper dragged Jaime by the shoulder in the opposite direction.

"Go get the bucket!" he repeated. "Don't dawdle." His shoulders were broad with the heft of an overlord. I knew my place and meekly went to obey him. I grabbed the bucket and stomped through the purple gayfeather and goldenrod, busting their blooms into the dirt.

"No, fool. Fill it first! Why would I need an empty bucket?"

I turned quickly and nearly ran back to the trough, but a few yards before I reached the barn, the town came to a queer silence. My publisher dropped his hands to his sides, puzzling a look from the horse to me and back again. People in the road halted where they stood, turning their heads in confusion. In a single second, all noise was sucked from us, and out of this quiet blew open the deepest thunder I had ever heard.

Down the narrow alley the walls of both buildings exploded, splintered planks blasted and crashed to the dirt. Hundreds of frantic starlings whirled to a crazed ball in the sky, and heat from the surgery poured into the street. I bolted with the others, racing across cracked glass for shelter, but the road beneath our feet rocked, and we could not escape the jacking, groaning earth or the choking sweet stink of the air.

I fell against wood planks and shards that lay in the dirt, stretching my hand out to push back to my feet. As I did, a rig and driver stopped short beside me, the horse rearing up to the sky, pitching the cart onto its side. Hoofs and chains, wagon wheels and dust crashed about us, and the driver jumped to his feet grabbing the reins to pull his animal away from the tower of smoke and flames covering the back of the alley.

The street beyond exploded again and fire shattered the

windows. All around people bolted screaming while the head of the fire raged up from the basements and covered us in buttery smoke. Bodies lay in dirt and ash beside the stores, dying souls among them as well, and from where I knelt I couldn't tell the difference. I pushed to my feet, running toward the alley and the injured, and pulling those clear who breathed still. My lungs filled with smoke and heat while bells around me clanged to call hook and ladder men, but the alley was engulfed within minutes.

As I worked the pumps with the brigade, fathers came to me begging for their children, women for their husbands, all pleading with me to find the ones who had vanished. I pumped till my muscles swelled with pain, at last sitting defeated in the heat and smoke.

Hours later by the rise of the hazy moon, the streets were crowded with families and old men, with ragged children and merchants, all come to watch. I stared as the fighters sought Doctor Hunnicutt in the flames behind the tinder of his blue door, when across Soledad I saw the boy, Rufus Sams, weeping out the hot night by himself.

I walked to him and put my hand on his back. He shuddered as he looked at me, then stood and ran off to where the fire brigade was pumping steam to build water pressure for the hoses. He stood alongside them for a moment until one man shoved him hard away, knocking him to the ground. Rufus scrambled up and ran straight at the fiery buildings, stopping short of the blazing warehouse walls.

"Jaime!" he called, and then again. He watched the roof as it caved upon itself, and when the wood fell thundering into its own flames, he reached his hand straight into the fire, stepping toward the heat.

I dashed to where he stood and took him, covering his burned hand and arm with my jacket as he began to scream. I looked around the crowd. The noise of this child's agony was so loud, yet no one turned from watching the flames to this trembling African boy.

"I'll find help," I said. "You won't lose that hand."

Before he could answer me, Stella appeared out of the dark, folding her arms around him. She pulled her shawl from her shoulders and wrapped his hand in it.

"Stella," I said, "we must get him to a doctor immediately."

She looked from the child to me. "Don't be afraid, Rufus. We will see to you." Confidently, she smoothed the tears across his cheeks and knelt to his height. "Come now," she whispered. "Take a slow, deep breath." Her hands, so pale and slender in the day, shone now like porcelain in the firelight.

I took a step forward, ready to lift the child and make our way to the Sisters' infirmary, when Peter Olenbush limped through the bitter brightness and swept the boy up in his good arm. He looked down at Stella with those indolent green eyes, his crooked smile tilting to one side.

"It's fine, boy," he said, yet still staring at her. "You'll be fine. Let me tell you something, a story about a trip I once took to Glen Bolcain, to that clear water where the cress grows sweet and wild like weeds." Stella looked at Peter as he began to sing-song this tale about a land the liar had probably never seen, staring as though she had known his comfort all her life. And I, towing such a heartache, merely gaped at the shadows they left behind as they walked off down the road.

I watched the dying flames through the night until a swarm of flies rose from the fire trench, pink in the dawn light, cutting a path across what remained of the buildings.

CHAPTER 11

I went down to the waterside the next day, heading toward the orange fire glow where police and nurses and fire boys fought to save the injured or to clear them after they died. As I arrived at the marshy end of Soledad Street, smoky air choked the cool river sky, and I tied a linen bandana around my neck and mouth before moving into the wreckage.

A single section of wrought fencing remained, warped from the fire's heat. Alongside it lay the charred blue door of Hunnicutt's surgery, and behind, a skeleton of brick foundations. Trees, now only smoldering trunks, stood at the river end of the alley, and the warehouse walls were scattered in piles of crumbled caliche and cindered oak.

Inside these ruins waited the venerable Doctor Herff, stooped among four Sisters from the infirmary, all of them slowed by the long, dark hours of work. Their space had been swept clean of ash, and a long table lay before them. The doctor took a cloth and wiped the table, swirling the muslin, pink from the blood of the night's bodies, in small circles. Behind him remained a portion of the building that had been adjacent to Schmidt's warehouse, a jagged limestone wall looking oddly now like a row of broken teeth under a metal roof. From beneath this eave, out of a red opening that glowed like a demon's eye, emerged Stella, hunched parallel to the uneven ground, struggling to push a cart on which lay the body of a young boy.

I stepped toward her to help but stopped. When she reached the rusty light of day she left the cart and stood tall, smoothing the dark bodice of her dress. She walked on, following a path that had been cleared between the burned wood and fallen walls and broken bottles and shanks of flesh. She walked straight and held her head high, though her skin was smeared with ash and her face taut from the long night.

She made her way around a bloodied man lying on a nest of splintered wood while a nun knelt beside him, tearing furiously at his rags of clothing to get to the body before it became a corpse.

Stepping over a chunk of limestone, Stella walked through long shadows thrown by the tree trunks. She followed an open passage between people who had come to look for family or for friends. Beside the dead, we living lined her narrow path, straining to see this lone woman with the terrible strength, and seeing her pass, all of us silently bowed our heads.

When she reached the old doctor, she spoke to him briefly and turned away. Moving beyond a preacher who held a shiny brass cross above a heap of bodies, she came to me, her eyes bloodshot. She led me to the cart, and pointed to the body of the boy who lay on it.

"That poor child," I whispered, staring at his dried black flesh and blood-soaked rags of clothing.

Her shoulders trembled as she said, "He was my student. Jaime Sams."

"Sams? Rufus's brother?"

She nodded. "No one found Doctor Hunnicutt's remains so

Doctor Herff sent me to search for him. I found Jaime lying in the basement of the Schmidt stores. In a closet behind an iron door, caught between cartons of old papers." She wiped her face and stood straight again. "He was thirteen years old. A man, I suppose, to some."

"What was he doing there?" She shook her head and set her lips tightly together. Gently, she laid her hand on the cavern that remained of the child's chest.

"Stella," I said, reaching ineptly for her, my wretched eyes agape, but she pulled back.

"Rufus is alive, though. Peter carried him to the Sisters' infirmary."

"Olenbush? You let Olenbush take the little one by himself? How can you trust that man with the child?"

"Don't," she whispered. "Today is too hard."

In a chilled pause, she held her hands together as though preparing a prayer, but her fingers clenched like claws. "That iron door," she said so softly I strained to hear, "it was locked from the outside." She stopped as two thrashers, brown and slender, lit on the cart where the child's body lay. Stella watched them without moving. "What people would leave a boy to burn alive?" she asked at last.

I didn't answer for several moments but she trained on me, waiting for logic in a world of infinite harm.

"I believe Tom Broc might have a theory."

"I should hope so. He's the man sent to investigate this morning."

"And was likely one of the last to see the boy," I said.

"Why do you say that?"

All around us the sunlight was filled with ash and festering smoke. I shook my head, hard and determined like a wild hog, but the memory of the man and the boy in the alley remained.

She narrowed her eyes. "What's wrong, John?"

Of course I could not speak of what I'd seen, a random image on a night of tragedy. I couldn't say it aloud to Stella of all people, the teacher of these children, not without truth of some kind. "Only," I said, "that he's a good detective and was in the vicinity last night. That's likely why they assigned him."

She leaned forward, putting her weight against the cart, pushing it on toward the nuns and the doctor and the bodies in the clearing.

I heard nearby footsteps and turned to find Broc himself striding toward me from the river. "Where've you been all morning? I coulda used your help clearing the dead and all the rubbish."

I stared at him without reply. "Sixteen dead, twenty-eight dying, not counting the coloreds. You missed the hard work." He pulled a pencil and a small copper's pad from his breast pocket, wincing as he did. He opened it slowly and made a mark alongside others. "No, seventeen. I hear they found the older Sams boy." He looked across the broad crossroads to the exhausted workers and nurses. Resting his fingers on the nickel Colt in his shoulder holster, he said, "Can't dally with you, my friend. We'll be salvaging the rubbish left in Schmidt's warehouse for days."

"Any idea of the cause yet?"

His eyes widened and his jaw tensed. "Early days, though old Hunnicutt had loads'a shelves of combustible medicinals, and lit candles all around that surgery, all four corners. It looks like a wick might'a fell into his pharmacy. An explosion of that much ether'd be like a blast of gum dynamite across the alley." A chuckle slipped from the side of his mouth. "The heat burst the windowpanes and the fire must'a jumped the alley."

"So the dark night and all these dead come from that? Children were killed, Broc, as well as a man of a hundred years!"

"That news is no longer the news today." He stopped talking suddenly and lifted a hand to cradle his left side.

"Are you injured?" I asked.

"Nothing really. Only a nick from a falling roof tile. Had to bandage it myself, though. Where is Hunnicutt, anyway?"

"His body's not been found," I said.

"Well they best keep on lookin' for him." He pointed to a bracketed medical sign lying on the ground, the doctor's name spelled in flourished alphabet. "Hunnicutt better turn up alive. Rest of these Bexar healers're not worth an Indian penny."

"My publisher says this is the worst event ever to happen in this town. I'll be writing of the dead for weeks."

"Schmidt's warehouse is gone. The losses to merchants will be vast. Goods belonging to others and not entirely insured. That's the story you should write. In the town's economics lies everything. That's the story you should write."

"You sound like my father," I said. "Money is his religion."

"Well, he isn't wrong, is he? Profit's everything."

In the yard beyond us, cleared of stones and stubble, sat a large transport wagon, its box filled with bodies, and two large roans ready to pull. Stella had taken a place among the townsmen loading up the last cadaver, the child, Jaime Sams. Beside her slogged Peter Olenbush, his hat fallen to the dirt, his shirt lined with sweat and stains of blood.

Turning back to Broc, I asked, "So what perished in the warehouse, then?"

"Everything Schmidt's investors had put in his care. Goods filled to brimming." With his voice rising, he added, "You best get to your pencil and tell the tale of these financial losses instead of your spiritual hobnobbing with the stories of dead people." His brow tightened and his mouth twitched. He squeezed his hands to white-knuckled fists just as he had the night before with the Sams boy. "I need to get on and itemize what's left."

"I can help you," I offered.

"No," he said abruptly. "Don't need you for that. Besides, too many embers lingering in the rubble still for a gold-fluted Boston son like you." He turned before I could argue, and breakneck like a beast ran to the ruins.

A crater of fresh clay lay between the wagon and me, and as Olenbush hiked himself to the bench and took the reins, the horses began to bray. "Wait there!" I shouted, and sprinted across the warm red mud to the wagon. "I can help," I said when I stood beside Stella. "I may be wiry but I'm strong."

"You ever put a corpse under the ground?" Peter asked.

"Never." Beyond us at the back of the alley lay a plot of scorched dyer's woad smelling of bitter, burning onions. I pulled myself up to the seat. "But I can learn how to do it."

He teased the animals forward, taking us to the edge of the ravaged town. We stopped at Mullally's yard where sawyers piled green cedar planks and shroud linen beside the bodies in our wagon.

The younger Mullally strode across the dusty earth carrying a tin box under one arm. Passing it up to Peter, he said, "These are all the coffin nails we could spare. Lucky Broc had that load from the gulf or you woulda been dumpin' them bodies inta' bare holes."

From the smoky road I heard the scrape of light wheels and turned to see a small flatbed wagon driving toward us. On the bench sat Didier with a dark, determined face, and alongside him, Ayla and the *curandera*.

"Hold on!" he called, and pulled up on the old mule driving them. He jumped down and helped the women after, then took saddlebags and a large white cotton sack from the bed.

Ayla took the sack from him, and said, "Who knows how

long you'll be up there buryin' folks. I bet ya didn't even think of sustenance for yerselves. And *curandera* brought a little packet, too."

The other woman handed me a deep basket with a small, purple plume across the linen cover. "Not coming with you. But this saves all."

"Thanks to you," Olenbush said.

"There's bedrolls here, too," said Didier. "In case you're workin' through the night." He transferred the provisions to our box even as the lumbermen loaded the planks beside the bodies. "I'd be with you if I weren't so old," he said holding out one hand, and his skin was tanned and toughened to the color of peat.

"We'll be enough," I said while he climbed back onto the wagon bench with the *curandera*.

Ayla lingered beside us, her hair matted with the work of this hard morning, and at last she put the palms of her hands toward me, reaching to find my face and once touching, for a few moments held fast to my cheeks like to a rough birth cord.

When all was loaded, one of the lumbermen remained in the wagon box, knee deep in flesh and wood, lifting his hands in the air. "Bless them, Lord," he said, drinking the wind like it was milk. "And bless those of us left behind." He struggled through the dead limbs, climbed atop a side panel, and jumped down. "One day we'll know why our Father brought this calamity to our city."

Olenbush stared ahead watching the soft buck of the horses while the poor praying fellow looked to us for an answer. Nodding, I whispered, "Yessir," but Olenbush did not speak. Rather, he growled deep and low at the animals, urging them on.

As we took to the trail moments passed, empty of voice or

any tell except his cold stare at the horizon. At last, I said, "You took Rufus to the infirmary last night? Will he lose the hand?"

He pulled us up the path with care, until we lurched to a stop against a limestone rock. "Don't know. A Sister had a look, but Rufus ran off before the doc came. I'm hopin' he'll be safe in a warm nest somewhere till this is over."

"Does he know his brother's fate?"

"Can't say until I find him."

"What's your opinion about our disappeared doc? You think he perished last night?"

"I told you before. He's a slippery one." Peter drove us into gloomy shadows of the wild oaks, where a dew lark sang on a branch hidden above our heads. "Gotta lot of questions today, Johnny. Is that your newspaperman's education?"

"Broc's thought was Doc Hunnicutt's clumsiness with his chemicals might have caused the explosion. Might have perished himself."

"Well, I think our constable may be wrong." Peter smiled and said, "Remember, Tom Broc would suck the life from a salmon in a scheme that'd bring him two bits. Sure as sure he's got a plan involvin' our Satan doc." A fierce edge of light cut across the tangles of pigweed and bellbind before us. "Wheels're stuck now. We'll be chopping our way for a bit," Olenbush pulled a long vaquero machete from under the bench and jumped into the shrubbery.

"I'll gladly help if you have another tool," I called out, and he looked up from the tendrils and the milk of the stalks. Leaning over the bench, he tugged a canvas bag from under the planks, and from this he pulled a tarnished long knife with a hide-covered rump. Handing it to me leather first, he said, "As long as you don't slit my throat, Johnny. Suddenly I got an itch round my neck."

"Murder is not in my repertoire."

He stepped back and yawned at the sky, his face slack and gray. "Yah, I do know that, man." He hunched forward and began cutting the vines from the wheels and axle trees, and I followed his lead. When his fists were well-covered with sap and tendrils, he straightened himself and leaned back against the box. "Can't claim I never killed a man. But I never killed one who didn't need killing."

"You're the judge, then?"

"Sometimes there's only a small nick to make that decision."

The damp from the brambles had soaked my trousers with milk and dew, and I bent to shake the cloth from my shins. "Perhaps I came west unprepared, Peter. But my ignorance is not permanent."

"Johnny, you're a lad I always liked. Despite your lily bones." He climbed to the wagon bench, pulling himself first and once seated he offered his hand to me—but I hoisted up without help.

"I'd like to make peace," he said quietly. "If Stella's the only thing that's between us we can get past that." He looked away, snapping the reins across the horses' rumps, and in a voice louder than usual, called out, "Heigh ho!"

CHAPTER 12

We lined the sour-smelling bodies, adults and children, on the weeds of the outer graveyard row, and pulled the planks from the back of the cart, the wood so new a faint scent of camphor clung to it. By midday we had hammered up boxes for every soul we carried, and placed each in its coffin. I knew some of the faces, one a teacher from Stella's school, two were merchants, and three I drank with at the Silver King. One was a girl from the cribs I had visited, and all of them now were returned to clay.

Peter pulled out the sack of food, and we sat on a dead woman's granite pedestal, a dinner of dark loaves and beef shank between us. Atop that hill far above the orange haze of the city, the earth and sky were of the same wind and smell, and the sun shed the same white light as that of a winter's snow.

"How long does it take to dig one grave hole?" I asked quietly, looking at the soil and our food, both of similar color and texture.

Peter's glance was impenetrable, and he lifted the bread quickly from cool plinth to his lips. "Ground's not easy up here. Through the night we'll be workin', Johnny. But others will come help. And they'll be bringin' any more bodies they find in the rubble. Preacher'll say his prayers tomorrow." His voice was gentle with no trace of whiskey on his breath. His eyes tilted down at the corners, and he watched the purslane roots in the dry earth at our feet. "A terrible night," he said, as though warning of a coming fury and not a nigh tragedy. "All these people lost."

"Do you think it was an accident?"

"You seeking ideas for tomorrow's story in the *Light*?"

"Maybe."

A vague smile crossed his lips and he laid his hands flat on his knees to stand. "I think people'll be making up stories for years. Unless a witness comes forward, and Hunnicutt is not about to be that fellow."

"Hunnicutt?" I asked.

"Last one to walk the alley before it blew to smithers." He bowed his head beneath the branches of the madrone tree. Across one boot clung a knot of black beetles and he kicked out causing them to fall to the dirt. "Kinda newspaperman are you, Johnny? Why d'you think old Doc Hunnicutt has disappeared today? Maybe you're not curious enough for your trade, my friend."

I noticed that his woolen breeches had been torn by the day's work. He caught me examining them and shrugged. "Not a practical suit to wear for this job. But I didn't know when I stepped out with Stella last night what would be required."

"You've not been home since?" I asked, and he shook his head. I grabbed a rock from the dirt and rubbed it hard across the gravestone. "Maybe we both love her," I began, longing for my whiny voice to be strong and full. "If she chooses you, I will live with it. But you must tell her the truth about her sister."

Behind the grave pedestal grew a tree laden with berries

bursting their membranes. Peter pulled a cluster to his lips, the red juice trailing about his mouth.

"You never even sighted her sister, did you?" I asked.

His expression did not change and after a moment of silence he asked, "No?"

"How can I trust you if you won't even admit you never saw her. Tom Broc actually believes you killed her."

"You of that same mind?"

"I see no proof, so no."

The wind brought the tangy smell of the last cut of hay up the hill, and with it the far sounds of wagon wheels and men's voices.

"Constable Broc only discovers criminals when it's convenient." Peter paused, looking straight into the October sun and struggled to speak. He lifted sound from his throat, almost language, then swallowed it all down again.

"What is it?"

"You're partly correct, Johnny. I haven't told Stella all the truth I know," he grunted, blunt as a cross. "But you're wrong about her sister. And Broc, too. There're things I can't say to Stella." He lowered his eyes to me, deadly and calm. "And you can never tell her, either. Knowing would break her heart. Lucy came to town mad as a swan. No more'n a child, except for her delusions about being stroked by God. Worked a small crib on her own nickel, lived in it even. Always bolted her doors behind her, and in the streets she wore the same yellow frock day after day."

The distant sound of the wagon screeched to a stop.

"You visited the sister at her crib?" I asked.

His lookback was a reprimand. "I did, but not until Valentine's feast this year. Rufus brought me to her and said she needed treatment. *Curandera* had worried about going down the cribs that night so she sent the boy to me to go." He stopped to watch a hawk lunge along the far side of the hill. He moved his lips to speak but did not, instead hunching his shoulders forward like cast off prey.

"Tell me."

"Lucy's lying on her back on a narrow bed. Couldn't even stand. A dozen bandages were not enough. Her stomach was covered in dried blood and her arms pocked with bruising." He drew his lips tight, nodding and blinking. "When I lifted the girl she screamed. One leg was broke and hanging loose. She told us that someone had meant to kill her."

"Who?"

Above him the narrow trunk of the madrone had shed its white bark for red. From a low limb was suspended a grisly lace of gutwork.

Peter followed my stunned stare. "A custom here," he said softly. "Eating the afterbirth." Dried and browned from the heat, the cord was wrapped round a prickled stalk. "But that's old innards. No one'll be comin' to eat those ones now."

"Who tried to kill Lucy? And why?"

Shrugging, he leaned back into the shade of the madrone. "I carried the sister through the dark to *curandera*. She called out a lotta names to me on the way."

"Was one of those names Tom Broc?"

"Always, Johnny. Broc's on everybody's list."

"Where is Lucy now? Does she live?"

"I left her with Señora Sams."

"But that was months past. Where is she now?"

Without answering, he tossed a dark crust of his bread to the ground and immediately it was attacked by titmice flocking to his feet.

"I think you're unable to tell the truth," I said.

"Sometimes there's just too much truth to tell."

Down the path the men leaped from the wagon, stomping

hard through the dust. After, they marched in rough unison through the graves, the sun above high as the arc of heaven would carry it.

The first to arrive was tall as Olenbush but thick and slow. He whistled as he approached, rifle in hand, waving the others forward. Not one of the six men carried a shovel. Peter stepped from the shade and stood still as stone.

"What's this?" I called out. "You come with no tools?"

The tall man shrugged but took no steps toward us. Around him on a tumulus the others waited, surrounded by the black earth of the dead.

At last Tom Broc sauntered from behind them, shielding his eyes with a bent elbow. "I told you to choose better friends, John," he said and suddenly lifted his hand high into the air. Immediately, four men rushed at Olenbush, seizing him by his arms and shoulders, while a fifth brute came at me. Broc leaped forward, stoking dust into the sunlight. "Hold the reporter till we contain the other," he said. "I got no beef with you, John, but I'll take your shooter anyway." Sweat pasted his curly hair to his skull and he wiped at it, smearing filth across his forehead. Up the madrone tree the grackles pecked at the dried afterbirth. "This is insurance, is all."

The four men holding Olenbush forced him to his knees while Broc trussed his wrists and ankles. The copper lifted one foot and stomped down on Peter's spine, collapsing his body flat on the soil. "I counted over fifty of your victims so far, Deutschy, children and women as well among them."

"What're you saying?" I pulled free of the man who held me. "Olenbush didn't set that fire."

Peter lifted his face, squinting at Broc through the merciless white light. He stared hard and long, like a tracker at an old footprint. "You and I know the cause, don't we?"

"I got a witness," Broc said to me, ignoring Peter. "German

fellow says after the fire, he saw your friend here with old Doc Hunnicutt down Dolorosa Street. And one of the fire boys found a riding cuff belonging to Olenbush in the alley between the doc's and the warehouse." He pulled a book of cards from his pocket and read. "Charred leather cuff settin' in the road by the corner of Navarro and Commerce." He closed the book and struck it hard as though it was a heavy haul of primary evidence.

"Thought Olenbush woulda' been far traveled by now. No matter, we'll hold him here till we're done. Boys'll be rolling the bodies into their coffins down bottom of the north slope, and I'll be writing the names of the ones he killed to keep it all straight for the families and the sermon and the judge."

He looked down the lea lands, black like oil and untouched by little but the river and this harsh sun. "Leave the coloreds by the gate, boys. Maybe someone'll come up tomorrow to dig them in." He motioned to a man with a shepherd-thin body. "Pull Olenbush over to the wagon and get him in it. Watch him, though, while we bury the rest. Keep your rifle to ready."

The wiry lad opened his mouth then closed it quickly. He pulled at Olenbush's arms, inching my friend's body through the mounds of soil. When at last he reached the wagon, he put his right foot on the first step, then paused and changed his mind. *Left foot first,* their mothers would say, *yer right is unclean.* Starting out again he began to climb to the bench, left then right, with the deluded faith of the frontier.

"Olenbush needs water," I called up to him. "He's not had a drink for hours."

"No matter. He'll pass out soon enough," said the lad.

I jumped up the steps and grabbed his canteen, bending his fingers back until he groaned. He lurched at me, stubby hands jabbing toward my eyes.

I saw myself busting open, wild bone and flesh, shaking and sweating. I lunged, pushing him from the wagon box, headfirst down the planks. I yanked his rifle and kicked him, then struck him with the gun butt, twice, or maybe four times, until the scrawny fellow dropped unconscious.

I could hear the echo of worship songs from the others down the far hill, their music in the graves disappearing as the winds shifted. I took my dag and cut the kerchief from Peter's mouth, then sliced through the rawhide strips holding him. He drank from the leather-bound canteen, and poured what was left down his neck.

I coughed up phlegm and dust, and he glared at me. "What you did," he rasped, "in this country, it'll kill us both. I thank you, Johnny, but we must go. Saddles're in the box." He lifted one from our dray, and grabbed leather satchels and Ayla's white sack.

Never pausing to utter or think but carrying stolen guns and knives, truth swallowed whole, we rode down the long avenue straight at the north hills.

CHAPTER 13

We reached the old King's Highway in an hour, crossed it with the horses and walked deep into the forest where the surrounding oak trees were tall and thick as turrets. Peter led us toward the musty smell of damp earth until at last we came upon a clear tributary of the river. The animals cooled and drank in the dim light shifting through the spinney, while sickle birds cried overhead.

Peter squatted on the slick mud, cupping that cold fresh water to his lips.

"I'd like to know your plan for us," I said. "And why we're heading away from town."

"Need to figure out some answers before we risk going back." He stepped forward into the stream and watched the flow ducking and draking over his boots. "Beyond that, I got to fetch Rufus. I put him into hiding last night." He picked up a stone and tossed it at the thistles on the far bank, and the scream and scurry of a gray fox caused us both to stop short.

"How close behind do you think Broc will be now?" I asked.

He shrugged, his face neither timid nor roaring. "He knows

damn well I didn't start that fire and now we're gone he may just be lookin' for someone else besides me to blame."

I moved into the rocky streambed. Bending forward, I splashed the water across my face and wiped my cheeks clean of road dust. "Why do you say that?"

"He's as crooked as a dog's hind leg, Johnny. Always was the kinda man would steal your silver then accuse your neighbor of the crime." The surface of the stream split open as a heron, wings of silvery blue, planted its feet in the shallows.

The wind was up and Peter moved to the bank. "Better get on." His blond hair, still damp in the hot sun, fell across his face, and he combed it straight back with his fingers, showing a sharp jaw and narrow, anxious eyes. He coaxed his horse from the water and tightened its cinch. "I first met Tom Broc on the docks in Galveston. Watched him throw an African dock jimmy into the gulf for no good matter. We all knew the poor man couldn't swim."

"Coppers get Broc?"

"Couldn't. He was a Pinkerton then."

"And the longshoreman?"

"The rest of us saw the African sink a couple of times so me and another, we dived for him."

"The man survive?"

"For a day or two. Then Broc had him drowned for good."

We pulled our horses through the slimy bank up onto the trail again through the oaks and the cypress. "Not much farther now," he said.

"What's our destination?"

He didn't answer, but pulled a packet from his saddlebag and tossed a piece of hardtack to me. "This'll keep you a while."

We moved through the brush until we came to a glade surrounding a deep, gray sinkhole of crumbling limestone. Fifty feet down lay a shadowy black hole shaped like a man's head and big as a cow.

"We'll be spendin' the night in these caves," he said. "Take your ride on into the thicket, tie it up, and come back." I frowned at him. "In case Broc is following, don't want to lead him here. Go on. I'll do the same to the east and be waiting for you."

I returned and found Peter sitting on a dead oak trunk, hat brim pulled over his eyes and his head cocked to one side as he listened.

"Should we get down there before we lose all light?" I nodded at the sinkhole and the cavern at the bottom.

"We should not," he replied. "We should wait for the current residents to leave for the night feed."

"Residents?"

He didn't rush to reply. I watched two hawks hooking above the trees, circling and waiting against the early moon, when suddenly from the deep hole rose a funnel of Jesu's hell, tiny screaking winged creatures in their thousands, spinning up into the darkening sky like a tornado.

"Mexican bats," he said at last, and walked to the end of the broken log where one of the creatures had fallen and lay squirming in death. "Barely the weight of a Morgan dollar." He held it in the palm of his hand and stroked its belly gently while it expired. "Let's get on," he said.

We shinnied down the crumbling wall to a vertical cavern drop the height of a man. Peter jumped into the shadows and called me to follow. "It's a flat landing," he said. I sought his shape in the dark, and once I found it, lowered myself beside him.

We continued on our knees into a narrow and low corridor with walls so close and air so thick with ammonia I called out to Peter. "I can't see and I can't breathe! I need to stop and right myself."

"A few more yards is all, Johnny," he said and pressed on. Dampness and silence surrounded us, and eventually the shadows turned to a black so profound all the edges of the world disappeared. Then I heard him shuffle to stand, and I felt the air cool. "You can get off your knees now." I crawled forward into a larger space and sat with my back against the cave wall. "Stay where you are. I'll find the torch and get it lit."

A few minutes' hence, a dim halo rose before me, its crest in the center of the cavern with Peter, but the organs of its light flickered over the ceiling of the cave and over the outline of a small boy who stood in the center where the tunnels met. The child cried out and ran to Olenbush, stretching his scrawny arms around his waist.

"Where ya been?" he sobbed. "Thought ya left forever."

Peter handed the torch to me and put his hands over the boy's shoulders, saying, "Ah, Rufe, you know I'd not let you fend alone."

And then out of a dark corridor, limped a figure ringed by light, a pale blonde girl moving awkwardly forward carrying her own flame and dragging her left leg. A vertical scar extended down one side of her face. She smiled at us with a crooked smile and asymmetrical eyes.

Peter placed his bags in the soft dust. "We got more food. For all of us. We'll be restin' here tonight, but then I'll have to move you again."

She nodded and as she did her face dipped in and out of the torchlight, and for one quick second I thought I knew her.

"Rufus, take Johnny here to your sleeping quarters. I'll be there soon. I brought treatments from your ma for that hand." He lifted his head and looked about the cavern where rat-gray fungus clung to the walls. "Christ, this is no place for a woman and child."

"Safer than some," said the girl. Though her voice was high and sharp, the family lilt was unmistakable. Unwilling to move another step, I stared hard at her face in the shivering light. This broken girl caught my gaze, and her fiery green eyes widened. "What's wrong with you?" she asked.

"Are you Lucy?"

"That's me," she said.

I snapped my head round to see Peter watching me. And so gently, he merely nodded.

"So you've had the girl all along," I whispered.

He let his shoulders slump forward and drew a hand down his cheeks. "She's been struck hard, ya' know? Who else'll stand for her?"

"You had her down here all these months?"

"Mostly. She rested with the *curandera* until I knew to move her. Not many places safe left for her."

"Safe? From whom?"

"The one she fears most is that worm of a copper, Tom Broc."

The girl kept a brazen gaze on Peter and suddenly barked out, "What did you bring us to eat?"

"Look at her, Peter! She's obviously crazed, as I would be if I lived in these caverns." I stepped across the crusted mud and put my hand out. "Come child," I said. "You're safe now."

She drew back, and lifted the hem of her skirts to her lips, kissing the filthy yellow cotton.

"I have tamales for you, Lucy," Peter said. "They'll keep your belly till tomorrow morning."

"With carne?"

"Yes, child. How are you fixed for water?"

"Enough. I was hoping to bathe in it, though. Not sure we have enough for that." And cackling as though the skull of the earth had split, she added, "God's work to stay clean."

We followed Rufus from the large cavern to a darker one that held a broad basin of tepid, reeking water, the caustic smell of bat urine smothering us. Down the passageway iron hoops and old axles rusted along the cave walls and high above our heads, torchlight revealed the drawing of a bull's head made in red pigment.

"Who occupies this cave?" I asked.

"Only us tonight," Peter replied. "Always been a place for folks to get swallowed up, though."

We walked deeper and deeper into the maze of chambers and corridors until the detritus of humanity disappeared altogether, replaced only by a hard crust of ancient guano covering the walls and floor. Lucy limped heavily but at the final turn, she pushed past Rufus into a side cave scattered with filthy blankets and meal debris. She crossed the floor to the far wall and lowered herself into the shadows of a flat outcrop.

"Sit where you like, but first give me that food," she said, leaning back and closing her lopsided eyes. She waited with her hands outstretched, the joints of her fingers pulsing and urging us.

Peter set the lamp on the clay floor across from Lucy, and the wall behind her glinted from the flame. A large shape lay in the shadows, down the throat of the cave, dark and long like the fallen trunk of a tree, and covered with old wool cloth. He walked to it, touching it gently with the toe of his boot.

"Died in the night," Lucy said, sniggering deep in her throat. "No doc to save the doc."

"I figured he might," Peter said. He bent to examine the man. "His burns were deep."

"Who was it?" I asked.

"Hunnicutt." He pulled the blanket over its face. "Found 'im on his belly near Dolorosa Street crawlin' through the smoke. Lookin' for some restful corner, I expect."

"To die?"

"Men like Hunnicutt don't ever believe they're gonna die."

"Why'd you bring him here?"

"A dying thief will have his secrets. Thought to get a few outta him." He bent low and put his palm softly on Rufus's head. "Hunnicutt was the last man in the alley that night. He swore to tell me what he saw if I took him with me and Rufus."

"And did he?"

Peter opened the saddlebag and pulled two cornhusk packages from it. "Some." The doctor's body lay at his feet like a castrate, and Peter stretched tall beside it. "Enough." He walked first to Lucy and then to Rufus, handing them the food. "Eat, Rufe, and then I'll treat your hand. Is it hurting you much, boy?"

"A little," said the child.

Peter took the food from the boy's hand and unwrapped it for him. "Here, then. You must be hungry after that long night. These are from your ma." He squatted beside Rufus and put his arm across the boy's narrow, bony shoulders. His copper eyes wide, Rufus laid his cheek against Peter.

"Wait!" cried out the girl. "We're never pagans. Take hands now so I can ask for blessings."

And as suddenly as she shrieked, she now snapped her eyes shut and mumbled out a prayer to some jilted prophet.

When Rufus had finished, his breath grew shallow and uneven as though he might be saving it. Peter pulled a small jar from his saddle bag and dipped his fingers into its paste.

"What is that?" I asked.

"His ma's potions. Pounded oak bark boiled up and stirred with Indian meal and charcoal." He pressed this to the child's hand and secured it with a muslin bandage. Around this, he tied a piece of soft, beaten cow hide.

"Those burns are already better tonight." Peter smiled at the child and brought him closer. "You two get to sleep now while John 'n' I ready for our morning ride."

"Where will we head?" I asked.

Peter lifted one of the blankets and shook it clean, then spread it back on the cave floor for Rufus. "Well, that's what sleep is for, Johnny. To blast through the day and do some figuring."

CHAPTER 14

The next morning I followed Olenbush on my belly as the two of us slithered down the passage toward the daylight. He growled with pain as he inched along but never stopped moving through the darkness. When at last we reached the light of the sinkhole he stretched slowly to stand. A heavy rain had fallen in the night, and he leaned against the damp limestone. He took a step toward the trellis of thick branches we had climbed down the day before. Looking to the top rim toward the wet vines and slick rock wall, he shook his head slowly.

"We need to get our mounts and lead Lucy and the child out of the cave," he said.

"What about Hunnicutt's body?"

He shrugged. "Doubt if anyone'll find him down here before he turns to bones."

"We heading back to town, then?"

"Not yet. The boy's hand needs treatment and his ma told me about a Tarasco Indian west of here on the Medina River. Another *curandero*." He looked down at the mud, avoiding my stare. "One who's not a target for Copper Broc like his ma."

I pressed my lips together, remembering the man, lips curled and eyes wide, snarling at Jaime Sams in the alley the night before. A thousand times in my life I would conjure that image, the child I might have saved had I not stopped to obey my publisher with his damned bucket of water. The truth and myth of that moment, of me, have fused forever.

"Stella found the boy's body behind a locked iron door," I said.

"Yes," he replied. "I know that." He put both hands flat on the mud wall, slick and soft like black butter, and shifted his torso forward to climb.

"And before the explosion, I saw Broc standing in the alley with Jaime Sams."

For a moment, I thought I saw Olenbush tremble. He turned to face me, pressing his flanks back against the wall, but suddenly he stepped forward across the jellied earth. "Harm is our copper's summer sport."

"A man who would give a child that kind of death has no purpose but evil."

The rising sun crossed his face with scars of light. "Oh, he had a purpose. He made that clear with Lucy."

"What purpose is that?"

He shook his head and in a voice brittle as straw, said, "One child dead, a girl nearly killed, and the warehouse gone. The only truth we got is Lucy, and she's been lunatic all these months."

The brush at our feet moved as a rat snake exited the cave. We watched it for a moment, listening to the red-tailed hawks hunt high over our heads.

"Snakes love those tiny cave bats," he said. "Just lyin' in wait for 'em to come home. While the chickenhawks mob up and wait for the snakes."

A smell of rot wafted slowly from the direction of the

cavemouth and I turned to see Lucy, crawling out and spreading her arms across the wet earth to reach for the light.

"Thank the Lord for our deliverance!" she exclaimed, and sat on a muddy rock.

"We're not delivered yet," I replied.

She angled her head and gazed at me. "The Lord knows I won't ever be free, all that I've seen in this town." Scrambling to stand, she held her skirts above her knees. "Look," she said. "I've scraped my skin off and need tending." Covered in dust and mashes of guano, her face as dark as blood, she pointed one toe forward like a shabby dancer, exposing the curve of her calf and its scratches.

"Where's Rufus?" Peter asked.

"Look at my leg!" she cried.

He stood, spine straight. "Johnny, can you fetch Rufe outta the cave on your own?" I nodded and moved to the mouth where the gorse smelled of fresh-cut vanilla. "Mark the walls like Hansel as you go in, and if you turn wrong, just call out. The boy'll hear ya. I'll take her up and bring our rides round."

"When are you planning to tell Stella you have Lucy alive?"

"Look at the girl. What's happened to her'll break Stella's heart." He pulled a deep breath. "Not sure I have the mettle in me."

I knelt in the scrub surrounding the cave entrance, damp from the rain and concealing cress and carrion, a swirl of flies drifted thick over the scumwater.

"You need a plan for her, Peter. She's not light cargo."

The stark sun pierced through the oak branches high above us, throwing half his face into blinding white. "The only plan I have at the moment is to keep this girl alive."

~

The boy crawled before me through the putrid dark corridors, until we came at last to the mouth of the cave. He stood in the daylight, whimpering quietly as he held his palm to his chest.

I moved alongside and put my hand on his scalp. "That hand worrying you, Rufus?" He shook his head. "Well, you get on my shoulders and we'll climb up together. Use your left hand when you can, and hold your right one safe from more harm."

Up and up we inched through the damp vines, heading for the light and the churchy sing-song of the girl at the top. About ten feet short we heard a man's drawl, deep and slow.

"Yah, girl!" the voice shouted, and I gripped the outcrops to hold us immobile. "C'mere ta' me, girl!" Mumbles then, and silence till branches broke over our heads while chunks of sour loam fell across us. Rufus bent to me and closed his eyes, the pods of his eyelids trembling.

Lucy began to bellow, at first low but her voice rose fast and fierce as a panther's scream.

"Y'all alone out here?" the man called out.

"I'm afraid," whispered Rufus, and I put a palm over his lips and shook my head to quiet him.

I heard skin slap skin, followed by thuds striking flesh. A large weight hit the ground, and I pushed the boy's head into a deep crevice for protection. Breathless, we waited, hearing only the sound of a dead load being dragged across brush.

"You killed him!" Lucy shrieked.

"Either you or him," came Peter's reply. "Quick, Johnny," he called down the sinkhole. "Grab the man's horse for the girl and let's be gone. Broc's deputies'll be scouting closer now." He peered into our abyss and seeing it clear, kicked the body down.

CHAPTER 15

Once on the Medina marshes we followed the bank to a line of bald cypress thick with sweet river scent. Peter had tethered Lucy's ride to his, but suddenly she pulled up hard on the animal, halting them both.

"What the hell you doing, girl?"

"Horse needs watering!" she called out.

"We been on a slow trot for a small hour, Lucy. That horse is fine."

"Well then, I do," she replied and dropped from the saddle to the slobland weeds, limping to the river.

He sighed hard and leaned over to dismount.

"No," I said. "I'll go. You still look to be in pain." I moved to the water's edge where she stood, legs planted, staring at me with huge eyes. Beside me lay a dead woodchuck, sticking partly to the mud while the rest of its body drowned in the seeps of the rains.

"What did you do to that animal?" she shrieked, and pointed to the decomposing chuck. "You stay away! All a' you! Just killing all that's joyful in God's sweet world." She knelt, leaning into the current, and began swimming toward the far bank.

"Lucy!" I called. "I did nothing to that woodchuck! It's long lay dead." But she only turned her head in my direction and seeing my worry, smiled.

Peter slid from his horse and ran toward her, but I was quicker and closer. I dived into the cold, clear river and pulled toward the girl through the wrinkles of light on the water's surface. Close to the far shore, I reached out and caught her.

"I won't go back! Scribbles and numbers're worth more than my life!"

I took her under the arms, her eyes burning and her body thrashing as I began to drag her back.

Once on the bank, I pushed her to the mud and lay beside her panting, my hand never releasing her arm.

"I could've got away," she said, "but I forgot all the tricks I learned on the Gila."

Peter walked close and squatted beside her. "Why would you want to run from us? It was you told me Tom Broc tried to kill you. Well, he's still hunting, wants to finish you off this time."

She leaned over her legs and began to rock side to side. "Didn't see anything! Don't know none of it."

"We must keep on," Peter said. "I'll take the girl with me. You ride with Rufus and bring Lucy's horse."

She wrenched hard away, but a moment layered with breezes rose about us until she sat quite still, suddenly staring wild-eyed at the blue-green surface of the river. She began chanting a hymn for the dead animal, quietly at first, then singing loudly and without melody, the words flying around us. "Sparrows sold for pennies, but not one creature is forgotten by the Lord!"

"What could have caused this poor child to lose her reason?"

"Came to town bedeviled," Peter said. "Tellin' people she heard voices of the dead round her, hoardin' food. Preached in the rain and bedded the local boys out in the bogwater for naught more'n a sack of taffy." He stopped and looked to her. "Broc arrested her once but let her go. Within a few weeks, he beat her near to death and left her locked in her crib box till Rufus and his brother found her."

He stood and offered his hand to her, and she, docile and still damp from the river, followed him to his mount. He lifted her into the saddle and climbed after.

"Why would Broc do such a thing?" I asked. Hoisting myself up behind Rufus, I added, "I guess I don't understand the makings of these frontier devils."

The sky had opened out to blue with dingy clouds straggling, and Peter glanced at me without moving. Finally, he said, "Hold the boy close and firm, Johnny."

I put my arms around the child and whispered, "We'll be another few hours then you'll have relief, son."

He nodded without turning to look at me. "Where're we goin'?"

"To get you medicines."

We rode along the narrows through foliage thick with large flying insects. Some paths were so overgrown they were nearly impassable, and deeper on we saw a few Tonkawa farmshacks set back against the forest in a small clearing. I scouted closer to examine one of the huts, a crude structure of mud pasted on loose wood, uninhabited now.

The light was failing and I called to Peter, "Could we stop here for sleep?"

"We're nearly to our destination, Johnny," he replied.

In another hour, I saw glitter across the river, bright flashes unlike that cast by the moon, and soon through the cypress trees we heard low, soft singing. Closer on, I realized the voices came from the far shore, and closer still we halted in a swampy, overgrown bog before an uncovered bridge hammered out of rough logs. Pounded deep into the marsh was a pole. At its top was attached the carved head of an animal so primitive in its artistry I scarcely recognized that it was a donkey's snout pointing straight at us.

"Why bring us here?" Lucy asked. "The Lord will strike you with madness and blind you on this river."

Peter ignored her and said to me, "Never mind the bridge. The riverbed isn't deep. Step your ride carefully, though. Horse could break a leg in the tangle and stones." He moved on and again I followed without question, the deep sweet smell of cypress rising above the sour water. A muddy path lay on the far bank, and we followed through thorned mesquite clusters until we arrived at a small hut built at the bottom of a grassy slope.

A dark-skinned man carrying a lantern stood on the hillside, beside him a woman, and between them a hound. She wore a plain dress, undyed and unfestooned, and her skin was pale as though coated in moonlight.

"Do you have sick ones?" she asked, and put her fingers gently on the brow of the dog at her side.

"A boy," Peter said. "A young boy caught in a fire."

A melody played by flutes rose from behind their shack, minor notes in a strange and precious lullaby, and all of us looked toward the sound.

"Bring me the child," the man said, and he squatted in the grasses beside a clutch of dying mustard plants. The woman came slowly toward us, timidly like a trespasser might.

I lifted Rufus from my horse and we approached. "Are you the *curandero*?" I asked. He was younger than I had imagined, his face and hands smooth, his eyes full of force. "The boy is in great pain. If these burns had happened to me, I would be howling."

"He is stronger than you," the man said, and turned to the

child. He took Rufus's injured hand but didn't pull the bandages away. The *curandero*'s heavy forehead and broad eyebrows furrowed, and alongside the lantern his fleshy round nose and cheeks pulled the light. "I will work on him," he said. "It will take many days."

"You haven't seen his hand," I said. "How do you know you can heal it?"

The *curandero* ignored me and said to Peter, "Give him."

The woman stepped forward. "We'll take the boy inside. The rest of you sleep out here."

Lucy had struggled from the horse and now stood with us, her lopsided face twisted in the ghoulish light.

"What is wrong with that woman?" the *curandero* asked.

"An accident," I replied. "Long ago."

Peter put one arm gently across the child's shoulder. "The boy knows more than he should so keep him safe. His name is Rufus." Pointing to the sky, he said "Look at those stars, son. They call that line the Seven Sisters."

The *curandero* studied me, and with his index finger drew a triangle in the air. Quickly, he turned his back and walked toward the hut, followed by the woman.

"Bring the child," she called over her shoulder, and Peter led Rufus through the dark drape covering the doorway.

They had taken the lantern, leaving Lucy and me in darkness cut only by a slice of moon and the thin light of Venus.

"Where are we to sleep? I'm cold," she said.

"We'll be fine. As soon as we get the fire up."

She squatted, monkeying herself down into a grassy nest while I sought brush and chunks of bark. I'd brought the phossy matches from the cave, and struck them now to flame.

I pulled bread from my satchel, and a packet of what remained from the cave meal. "Here, Lucy," I said. "And a little water, too."

She took it all, piece by piece, mouthing thanks in the starlight and staring at me as she curled forward across the cradle she had dug in the earth.

Long into the night, the silent part when even the panthers sleep, I awoke to Olenbush sitting beside me.

"Is the boy afraid to be at the house alone?" I asked.

"No. Other children're sleeping beside him. And it's warm. They even fed him some *churpo* soup, all chili'd up with turkey and corn. He'll be fine for a time."

"And his hand?"

"*Curandero* is confident in his own talents." Peter stepped forward to extinguish the last embers of our camp, grinding his boot heel until firesmoke and the sweet smell of roasted wood were all that remained.

I sat up and pulled my jacket around me. "San Antonio is a shambles of a town, ghosts and criminals guarding their inches. Not all so different from Tampico."

"Or Boston?" He stared at me after he said it, his smile slipping awkwardly.

"I'm sorry, Peter."

"For what?"

"That I never believed you."

He shrugged. "We're all the same. Just lookin' to leave our markers on the ground before arrivin' at the grave."

Lucy watched us from the other side of the fire pit. In a strangely calm and lucid voice, she asked me, "Am I your sister?"

I held my breath and felt the forest close around, our camp and our crimes and even our forebears. As gently as I could, I replied, "No dear."

"I know that I'm someone's sister. I remember that." She closed her eyes and in her dreaming, said, "I threw my sister to her bed. She's still sleepin' there, I suppose. With the other insects of the Lord."

A noise from the dell brought us all to stand. The night was vast and otherwise quiet until the rain began to fall on the fleeces of our bedding. Peter bent to shake the drops from Lucy's spot, and as he did he whispered, "I guess it's time for me to fetch Stella."

CHAPTER 16

I slept close to the river, waking at dawn to a forlorn mockingbird searching for its pitch. I sat up to pull the horse blanket around my shoulders and saw Lucy standing in the shallows of the riverbank. She bent forward, cupping her hands together to dip light from the water, then stopped abruptly and stepped out into the channel. She stretched tall, wrapping her arms around her chest, and under the breaking day, she was stiff and pale as Bathsheba.

"That icy river water'll get into your bones," I called out, worrying I might have to dive in to keep her from running again. "You'll end with winter fever if you're not careful."

"This is God's palace," she muttered, and lifted her sodden boots high as she made her way back to shore.

Peter stood beside our charred firepit. He took his bedroll from the damp earth, shook it out, and handed it to her.

"You're shivering, child," he said, and he picked up a darkened stick, one too tough to burn. "Here, hold this in your hands. It's still warm."

She took it from him, turning it over and over like a puzzling penny until her fingers were grimy with soot. She giggled hard and looked at him, the expression in her eyes old and fierce.

"What could have brought her to this?" I whispered.

"Fell to the pleasure of the Lord too young. You know how that ends for a girl, don't you? Every door she opened showed a brute Jesus and she trusted 'em all. Broc left her for dead, but if she survives, he won't be the last."

As he spoke, three young boys crested the gully hill, laughing and racing around us.

Peter pointed to a shoeless child in a plain white shirt and baggy pants. "Our boy is feeling better."

"Hardly recognize him," I said. "Cheery little fellow today. What's he wearing?"

"The woman gave him clean clothes. She burned the others."

"A smile from that child gives me peace," Lucy said and I whirled to face her for the voice she used was calm with flattened vowels, altogether not the girl I had met in the cave. "Don't you think?"

Before I could speak, Rufus called out, "Mister Olenbush! Mister Ives! Miss Moore!" He ran toward us and sat in the grasses at our feet. "Look, I have new friends!"

He waved at the others, his injured hand wrapped in unbleached linen, and I said, "Be careful, Rufus. Don't worry your wounds any more than you need." I squatted beside him. "How is your hand feeling?"

Rufus grinned. "Can't feel nothin' anymore."

"*Curandero* spread paste on it last night and the child slept," Peter said.

"Will he lose it?"

"A *curandero* would never take it off."

Suddenly, one of the boys shouted, "*Andale!*" and they all

bolted fast down the hill to the hut, calling to each other as they ran.

"The woman will feed us," Peter said, and together we three headed down the slope, the horizon glowing with the orange light of dawn.

Our host, El Niño Adelano as he was called, sat at a rough table near the open doorway of the building. Beyond him lay sleeping mats and beside those, a broad circle of blue and red beads had been arranged like a necklace on the dirt floor. In its center lay the bleached bones of four cow mandibles.

"Come," he said, and gestured to benches beside him. "She brings food. Children ate before daylight."

Within moments, the woman swept through the back doorway carrying a clay plate of roast corn and squashes mixed with red chili peppers. She wore a dress of bright yellow cotton with black trim. Wrapped around her hair were scarves of the same colors, glowing with the sheen of silk in the dim light. Hurrying, she pushed aside the musty table clutter, narrow sable brushes, a book half-eaten by moths, a brass wick trimmer, and a cluster of broken eggshells. When she laid the plate before us, steam rose from the vegetables, filling the small room with the tarry, tangy smells of *epazote* and mint. Adelano ate without speaking until no food remained on his plate, and then mumbled to the woman and rose from our table.

"What did he say?" I asked.

"No idea." Peter shrugged. "Don't understand more than a coupla' his Indian words."

The two walked toward the door and waved us to follow them into a narrow passageway out the back where we found a smaller hut, a mirror of the first in construction. Much of its sod floor had been dug to a large pit about two feet deep and this burned still with roasting rocks and flames, while around it was a black circle of carbon stain. On one side lay a midden of decomposing bones and shells and dung, and on the other, in the far corner, stood a brass urn the size of a man. The pelt of a large rabbit stood alongside, stuffed and remolded into the stance of a living creature that appeared to watch us with glass eyes.

Adelano took a small, dark medallion from his pocket and walked to Lucy. He lifted her hand and roughly opened her clenched fingers, spreading them and placing the medallion in her palm.

"You are sick with many inside," he said. "This is the sign of Juan Matha. He will help your ride home."

"I have no home!" the girl howled, and moved wildly toward him.

Adelano didn't shift or pale, but said calmly, "Now you are a slave. Juan Matha is holy and will break your locks." He took the medallion from her hand and held it up to her. "He was not a man. Much stronger than men." He thrust it to her and strode to the far side of the fire.

When he returned, he held three chicken eggs. He began rolling one egg across my face and arms, my chest and legs, until he had touched my entire body. He handed the egg to the woman who cracked it into a clay cup. Adelano continued with Peter and finally Lucy, and when all three of us had been stroked with the eggs, the woman emptied the cups in the fire and nodded.

"Go," she said and turned her back, and we went out into the day.

By the late afternoon calls of the wrens, I found Peter behind the small hut. He had packed his ride and stood alongside our most capable horse.

"Where are you going?" I asked.

"To see Stella."

"You choose this day? You won't be safe in town yet."

He shrugged, cinching the leather straps tight around the mare's belly. "I'll be bringing her back tonight."

"But if you're caught, Broc'll have you killed," I said.

He let go of the saddle and turned to me. "I need to know she's safe. The only sure way is to have her with me." Lucy came upon us then, lugging a great basket filled with long-wicked candles on her way to the scullery doorway. "And you were right all along. Stella should know what became of her sister."

"You leaving us?" she asked. She wore a torn dress of green cotton, full from neck to ankles with a bone button at her throat, and across her bodice dangled the medallion from a heavy black chain. "Will you return?"

"To be sure," he replied.

Lucy shook her head. "I doubt that. Why would you return if you can escape?"

I walked to his side and took the horse's reins. "I'll go," I said. "I've more chance to survive than you."

Peter blocked the mare and waited for me to move away. His eyes were focused and annoyed, but I faced him without moving, both resolve and friendship sticking in my gullet. As we watched each other the small muscles around his mouth began to twitch and his brow, so determined a moment before, creased in curiosity at me. At last, he stepped back from the mount, and I lurched up into the saddle.

"Now, where are you going?" Lucy demanded. "And the other is staying? You men are so confusing to me."

"Do you remember someone named Stella?" I asked, but she shook her head again.

"Don't be working your way through town in the daylight," Peter said. "And don't dawdle. Go to the school, tell her the truth, and bring her out."

The truth, I thought, without smiling at the irony.

"Yes, the truth," he replied, and I realized I had spoken the words aloud. "Everything."

CHAPTER 17

The Fernando bells tolled as I reached the ditch at Hondo Pass, and with the last chime, I knew the chili queens would already be selling supper to the crowds on the plaza. I tied my linen kerchief around my mouth, pulled my hat down, and avoiding the road into town, followed the watery *arroyo*. Taking the horse judiciously, I trod like ghostbones through the twilight.

At Guenther's flour mill, the sun had dipped below the horizon and a dying yellow glow spread across the grinding house. All lay still but for swollen vermin darting across the work yard, and I paused to scrutinize this odd calm. A single soul, an old man, exited a white wood door and turned toward the sound of my mare's shoes clacking on the road. I nodded but the man only stared, frowning even, and scurried toward his horse. In his arms he carried a checkered hat with large red horns, much like the crown of a joker devil. Once astride the animal, he centered the hat atop his skull and trotted on without acknowledging me.

No horses were tethered for the length of King William Street, the storefronts gone dark, and the usual end-of-day ruckus completely extinguished. At the Presbyterian Church two men rushed past me, galloping toward the corral. I heard the cellar hatch open and close, followed by the nicker of horses.

I peered into the yard. A dozen rides waited, their backs glazed with amber lamplight. None was being watered or fed; none settled in while their master accepted the commandments of the Lord. I pondered the meaning of this until I noticed the restless Morgan bay belonging to Tom Broc, a long, thick work rope coiled from its saddle, and another hat of handmade horns hanging from its sidepack. My mare snorted loudly, and I, growling low, admonished the animal and turned quickly from the churchyard.

I found Stella at the Rincon Road Freedmen's School, that neglected limestone building on the scrappy south bank of a riverbend. She worked alone in a first-floor classroom, the children and other teachers gone. I watched her through the bubbled windowpane as she extinguished the wood stove, her cheeks paled to gray and her hair disordered. She carried a rifle and leaned it against the inner door jamb, pausing to strike a match against the falling light. Her eyes were pure torment.

I thought to tap the glass, but not wanting to frighten her, instead I led my horse to the back of the school and climbed the broad steps. She stood in the hallway holding the rifle and now a lamp as well.

"It's me," I said. "John."

She lifted the lamp high to see my face, her hand and the flame trembling. "At last," she sighed. "Are you harmed?"

I took the lamp and gun and put them on the desk. "I'm fine," I replied. "I was heading for your rooms but saw the light. Why are you at school at this hour?"

She slipped her arms around my shoulders, and the musky smell of chalk lay on her clothes. She stepped closer, leaning toward me until I felt her breasts against my damp shirt. "I worried so after you. Where have you been these past days?"

She carried the sweet smell of cedar smoke and I flushed, couldn't move or speak but inhaled the lure of fragrant wood on her skin. I closed my eyes and held my breath, brushing my lips across the rough wool of her dress like a thief in the night.

"I've come to fetch you," I said at last.

She stepped away to look at my face and took a deep gulp of air. "You heard about the threats to the school, then?"

"No. Who threatened the school?"

"Two men came here to tell us they intend to keep these children from schooling. In the middle of the day! In front of our students!"

"Did you know them?"

"Of course. They are all neighbors," she replied, sighing.

"Why would they do this?"

"Don't be naïve, John. You know why very well. And just after Schmidt's fire, people began saying that Peter and the Sams family caused the explosion. Early yesterday morning someone ransacked the Freedmen's Bureau."

My lips were dry, my throat as well. "The streets are dead quiet tonight. You shouldn't be alone here."

"That's why I have my mother's gun." She put her palm around its barrel, tapping the steel with her fingers.

"Come with me, please. These men are fiends."

"They'd never attack a white woman," she said, waving a hand through the shadows as though scrambling mayflies. "As long as I stay in this building, they won't harm it. They're cowards who battle with children." Her voice rose harsh and hoarse, and she glared at me.

The light from the lamp curved across her shoulders, and I waited for her righteous anger to ease, until we stood quietly studying one another.

At last, she asked, "Do you have news of Peter? Constable Broc says he was killed escaping, but I don't believe it." She untied her apron and held it bunched in her fist.

"He's well. And I've come to bring you to him."

"Thank God!" She wiped the apron across her cheeks and eyes. "Last night I saw the police watching my rooms. I told them he didn't set that explosion. He was with me when it happened." Taking my hand, she said, "You're covered with road dust. Come, there's fresh water in the cookery."

In the kitchen we stood beside the cistern, and she handed me a long-handled brass dipper. I filled the bowl, lifting its floating light to my lips.

"Rufus is gone," she whispered. "They shot at his mother in her home, and the boy hasn't been found."

"Rufus is safe with Peter."

Her eyes welled; I should have touched her then, reached for her, but I only replaced the ladle in the water, the brass cracking against steel like the shatter of ice. "Who shot her? Where is she now?"

"She died in Doctor Herff's surgery this morning." Stella paused, and brushing breadcrumbs from the table with her fingertips, she added, "A whole family removed so easily just like barn rats. You wouldn't think it possible."

"Not the whole family. Rufus is still alive."

She drew back a step, and without shifting her gaze from me, she nonetheless stood so far, at the dark edge of creation where everything comes to end. "He's an orphan now. Can't return to this town. He'll be lucky to finish his life on a farm as some little henhouse boy, never learning to do sums and forgetting how to read."

I walked to the window and stared at the road. "If they watched your rooms, they could be watching you everywhere. The streets are so silent tonight and just now I saw a dozen horses at the Flores Street church, a dozen of them packed and ready. Tom Broc's was among them."

"A fire for a fire, that's what the men said when they came here."

"We must leave quickly!"

A beam from the far road caught her eye and she leaned back, balancing as though at a ledge. "I once saw my mother hold a rifle on some men who'd come to stop us burying a slave. Just after the war when no one was meant to be slaving anymore, our neighbors still hanged whoever they caught. And my mother, all alone in our fields, found this old Negro man on our land, hanging from a sycamore by the river. She got all us children to help her cut him down, dig his grave, and when the Knights of the Golden Circle showed up to set fire to his body, she raised her rifle at them."

She replaced the lid on the water tank and folded her arms across her breasts. "No one in my family has ever looked away and I'm not leaving now." A far-off dog barked and Stella turned. "We live in a city with a great many coppers and wards. Even if Constable Broc is rotten, others aren't. The faithful will always rise."

"Perhaps, but perhaps not this night." She scowled indignantly, and I, a boy never quick enough or strong enough, never one to fight when others bullyragged me, I said boldly, "You can't stay among these people."

"How can I leave the children? How could I go with you and leave them behind? Who would take my place now and teach them to read and to write?"

A rusted weathervane squealed, and like a lunatic compelling a dream, I blurted, "Peter has found your sister! He's waiting for you, with Lucy and Rufus down on the Medina. Please, Stella, you must come now!"

She stared for several moments as though she hadn't

understood, her chest shaking as she tried to right her breathing. Then so deliberately, she extinguished the lamp and we stood in the violet dusk, fooled in the dark to thinking I heard far-off voices through the shiver of breezes.

"Are you certain it's Lucy this time?"

"Yes," I replied. "He found her, the girl in your picture. There's more, but we must go quickly."

She took my hand. "Please," she said. "Take me to her."

We set off behind the convent's infirmary with the sound of the black herons barking down the deserted river. She sat astride and pulled close to my spine. Her arms clenched around my chest, the urge of her body warming my back. She pressed her face on my neck calling questions into my ear though we moved at a gallop and I understood none of them. Yet as the November winds fanned cool past my cheeks, I knew those few moments before we reached the limits of town would forever be my wildest.

Back past the lower mill road, I slowed the horse to descend into the arroyo, and Stella shifted. I felt her body turn and tense.

"Stop, John! Dear God, please stop!"

Pulling the horse up in the muddy bed, I put one arm around her. "Are you hurt?"

"Look!" she said, removing her hands from my body and leaning to dismount. She pointed to San Antonio where a fantail of sparks lit the black sky. "It's the school."

The white glow of a far-off fire smeared over the stars. "How do you know?"

"The klansmen. There'll be no more learning for my children now!" The wind had come up, and she stood beside the horse, clinging close to it for shelter and staring at the night horizon until I took her hand.

"We should go," I said, but she pulled from me.

"Did you know they keep the heads of the poor men they

hang? Rufus's father. His had full teeth even." Sweat rolled down her temples, her hands shaking. "In Doctor Hunnicutt's cellar on a shelf above the winter apples, until they paid Hunnicutt to boil the flesh out."

The firelight had dimmed, the sky lit now only by drifting white smoke. I reached for her again, touched her cool, clammy skin to lift her to our mare, and this time she allowed me.

CHAPTER 18

We crossed the donkey bridge in the deep night, long after the moon had spun its ruined light to seed. Once on the north bank, I squeezed my legs against the horse's flanks and let Stella slip to the spongy ground.

"Without hooves or breeze, this land is so silent," she said. "How much farther?"

Surrounded by brush oaks and tall river grasses, we could no longer see the curve of the far horizon or locate our place on the land. I swung around and slid down. I could turn a lie, I thought, and make this night last forever. We could be anywhere, standing at the shimmering surface of any of a hundred creeks. A blackthorn bush grew in the loamy bank soil beside me, and I plucked a branch from the heavier bough, ripping the wild fruit from it, and greedily hesitated to tell her we'd arrived.

"John?" she asked. "Please, how far are we from Lucy now?" Her eyes tilted down at the corners and had turned deep gray in the cool night. *So well-mannered*, I thought; *so gentle and kind.*

I tossed the wood to the ground, and its thorns left a smear of blood on my thumb and palm. "We're here," I sighed. "In the daylight you'll see a gully, and in that gully is the healer's hut. Lucy'll be sleeping now. Give me a minute and I'll find us dry ground and lay the bedrolls."

Before I could move again, a voice pressed out of the dark. "No lone man has ever spent a longer night." Peter trod toward us along the water's edge, striking a match as he approached. Neither drunk nor heroic, he stopped within feet of Stella, tapping one hand on his thigh over and again as he watched her. He held the light before her face until the flame burned his fingers. He dropped it to the mud and said, "Thank you, Johnny," and again so gently, "thank you."

I heard the rustling of Stella's petticoats as she took a single, tentative step toward him. She paused against the black of the insensate night, searching for the lines of his body. Before she could move again, Peter reached his hand out and touched her shoulder like a vein bringing blood to his heart. Neither spoke, but I saw their faithful shadows meet, and I, wretched glutton, dug deep in my pocket for the Lucifer box, sparked another light and held it up to reveal their urgent faces.

Turning from them, knowing and turning anyway, I took hold of the reins and led our ride down the riverbank until I was out of earshot. I'd reached an oak, squat and of my own height. Uncinching the saddle, I yanked it to the ground and spread a bedroll on the sawtooth grasses. The dark river obscured everything but the sounds of those two voices, man and woman, and their soft laughter, until finally I escaped into sleep.

"Mister John! Look!" I awoke into the autumn mist and its miserly sun, and stood quickly to Rufus's call. He ran toward me holding Stella's hand in his good one and pulled her beside him. "Miss Moore's here!"

Nodding to them, I bent to the river sand, cupping a fist of it to rub over my cheeks. When I looked up, dust glimmered over her face in the early light, leaving her skin gray as a mask.

A cloud crossed the sun and she shivered a little. Staring at me kindly, she said, "We five are a family, John, aren't we? You and Peter and Rufus saved my sister and I'll be grateful all my life." But even as she spoke of thanks, her eyes, red from the night, filled.

"How did you sleep—" I began, but stopped abruptly, flushing to think that this dawn my simple question might be an invasion of secrets.

"Well," she replied, though her face was drawn. "The air and the quiet remind me of where I was raised." Stepping closer to the boy, she clasped her hands over his shoulders and added, "Thank you for bringing me here."

"Have you seen your sister this morning?"

"Not yet. When Rufus found me, I was sleeping and Peter told us to come fetch you before we go down to the house."

"You surprise me."

"Why, John?" She bent to pull a clump of wild mint from the soil at my feet, shaking dirt and clinging worms from it. She smelled the broken leaves and slipped them into her pocket, stretching and gazing at me. "You think I should've run to her at dawn? We've sought her for so many years and now I'm afraid I might not be ready. We're funny sorts of creatures, aren't we?"

From down the gully, smoke began to spread, carrying the buttery smell of morning stew up our little dell.

"*Padrina* will feed us," Rufus said. "Come, Miss. Meet my friends. Please." He dropped her hand and raced down the slope.

"Peter explained the situation to you?" I asked, ignoring the child, and Stella nodded. "Then you know that she was beaten and left for dead by Tom Broc, our fine copper. Her leg broken in several places. Her left eye blinded by the blow from an iron rod and her cheekbone shattered. It never healed properly and what you might remember as a cherub's face is now a ghoul's. And this first-hand information came from your student, Rufus, who discovered her and saved her." I repeated these facts as though they could prove my worth, proudly even, and once begun, I couldn't stop. "Before that, she worked the bars, or tried to. She may even have a child somewhere. She has many injuries, dear Stella."

Her arms began to tremble. She clenched her hands together at her waist, but the knot of her fists still shook.

"Stella..." I said, and her cheeks had mottled with dark red blotches as though someone had struck her. "Lucy may never again be the girl you knew." I stood back to wait.

"Peter told me all this," and with her voice quavering, "but why do you believe I must hear it all again from you?" She turned and left me in the marsh weeds, arrested alongside the horse and the stunted brush oak.

"I'm sorry!" I called and stumbled after her. "I'm stupid and so unkind."

"You are!" She stopped on the slope, glaring at me through fresh tears. "Standing there so easily exposing my sister's story... well, this isn't the first time such a thing has happened to Lucy. My family's life went awry years ago."

Laughter of the *curandero*'s children shrieked up at us from the huts, and the call of a wide-winged owl fell from high in a sycamore. With the milky swirl of autumn sunlight caught in her hair, she said, "What a cruel man you've become. I only want to see Lucy safe. My mother and father will care for her once she's home. And you, in all your wisdom, can return to Boston or Mexico or wherever you travel next for your stories."

"It was not my intention to hurt you," I said. "I only wanted you to have the truth. So not to be shocked."

She shrugged and left me standing on the shaman's magical hill. And I, still such an indigent soul, finally understood that exercising power over another is, by its very act, the gravest weakness.

I found them all in the *curandero*'s home, a garrison of judges surrounding the breakfast table. Lucy stood alone by the fire, fingering the cross on rough rosary beads wound around her wrists. When her sister went quietly to clasp her, Lucy pulled away, tore the amulet free, and threw it into the fire.

"You won't master me!" she shouted at Stella and paced about the room, turning suddenly at each corner.

Stella followed, trying to enclose the girl again in her arms. "Don't, Lucy. You're safe now." Her wide gray eyes reflected the daylight, glistening with sudden tears.

Lucy pushed her back, standing straight, obstinate even. Stella stared at her disfigured face and costume. The torn lace collar hung from her throat, and the hemline of her dress fell only to her ankles, showing her bare feet.

Stella jumped at the sight of her sister's right foot, where three toes had been chopped away and deep purple scars sealed the flesh. "Who did this to you?"

"The man with the hatchet," Lucy replied.

"What man is that?"

"The self-same fellow," she said, her eyes bright. "But for the Sams boys, he would've severed my head instead of my toes." As the light spread across the sod floor, she cackled hard, a laugh from deep in her gut without any joy.

The *curandero* walked to them. "*Es susto.*"

"I don't understand," I said, but the *curandero* didn't look at me.

He stood beside Lucy, whistling low with the moan of an animal. Stroking her shoulders, he continued in this deep, airless tone until she squatted on the nearest bench.

"*Susto,*" Peter said. "Meaning her soul has left because of the harm done to her." Unbidden, he walked to Stella. "Healing Lucy will take many months." He took her hand and added, "What Broc did to her can't be measured in simple sin."

"But why would he hurt her like this?"

"A devil," the woman said. "The girl will never heal." She sat at the table and ate from a bowl of corn and broth, spooning it and then gulping the remains from the lip of the clay.

"My mother wouldn't agree," Stella said. "A soul doesn't disappear because of harm done to its body. A soul is eternal, brought to life by love."

"Don't trust your mother's god," said the woman. "That god is not a smart one." On the table beside her bowl lay a bleached knuckle bone. She grabbed it and handed it to Lucy. "Take it. *Curandero* gives it to you for your next journey." And to Peter she said, "You must leave us. The boy can stay, but the rest must take this girl and go."

"I'll not leave the child alone again," Peter said. "Ever."

"You'd evict us without cause?" I asked the woman.

"A girl without a soul will poison *curandero*'s work. What made her this half-devil?"

"A man in Bexar," Peter replied. "A jack of Satan."

The *curandero* spoke to the woman in their language, and turning to us she said, "You can stay one week, all of you in the yard, while the boy's hand heals more. Then go." She pulled her hair from her shoulders, tying it into a low bun, glossy and black. "Find shells in the river. Clean them and bring them to me. I will make strings to protect you." She walked to embrace Rufus, leaned over, and kissed his cheek. "You will grow to a fine man. Come to the house each morning for salve."

Then to Stella, she said, "You must feed your sister and keep her calm as long as you can. She will pass soon. And without a soul, she got no hope."

"Don't say these things!" Stella exclaimed. "My God, she can hear you. My family and I...we'll care for her."

The *curandero* glanced from Stella to Lucy, shaking his head and smiling gently. "A devil man has her. You can't save her."

Stella sat on the berm by the Medina River, holding the boy in her lap as she spread the *curandero*'s poultice across his wounds. I knelt near while her sister stood on the muddy bank staring at the water. Lucy wore old hobnail boots the Indians had given her, shoes of an incorrect size, thick-soled and treacherous, even.

"Would you like to see Mother?" Stella asked her suddenly. "Peter has offered to take you home, if that's what you want."

Lucy didn't respond, but stared at the thick stems of a tuber top growing wild in the soil at her feet. Finally, she bent to it, yanking hard to free it from the earth. Having succeeded, she dusted it clean and said, "I'll save this for our trip, Sis." She limped far into the tall weeds then, drawing her clean yellow bonnet close around her cheeks as she went.

Peter took a step toward her, but Stella lifted her hand to stop him. "Don't," she said. "Lucy won't run. She wants to go home."

"And you?" I asked. "You want to leave San Antonio and return home?"

"I'd like to see my parents." She looked directly at me. "I've no reason to stay on here now that the school is burned. The children will just scatter back to cropwork. I'll have nothing to get up in the morning for."

"You could teach at a white school," I said. "Why wouldn't you seek a position doing that? Plenty of new children moving in with their families."

"A white school would never hire me now that I've taught the Africans. If I stay, I'd have to give up teaching altogether. And I couldn't nanny, either. Dressmaking is all that's left for my livelihood."

Peter squatted next to her, and grinned at the child. "We'll all take Lucy home, Rufe. Even if you can't stay in town anymore, you got a home with us wherever we are. You ever been up the lines north of Bexar?"

The child shook his head but looked to Lucy who stood like a virgin under the elms, her fingers on the tips of the wild barley. "What about Mister Ives and Lucy?"

"Her parents will see to her," Peter said. He sat back easily into the lush silver clover, nestling alongside Stella while the faint sun streaked his eyes to gold. "We'll just be fetching a few items from San Antonio and then say goodbye to town forever. We can drop Lucy in Milam County at her parents' farm, and then be off to California. About time, I think."

Rufus thought about this watching the two of them in the clover, and finally asked, "Are you and Miss Moore married? Will you be my parents now?"

Stella lifted her head quickly to glance at me but it was Peter who answered the child.

"No, but not for want of me asking. If Miss Moore's secret heart will agree, and her ma and pa, then we'll wed. Maybe in Milam, darling? Will you say yes, finally?" She stared at the ground, but I saw the flash of her smile anyway. Only a glint lay between them, but the seal was clear. "And you, Johnny," Peter added, "will you come with us to Milam?"

I didn't answer Peter's question and he didn't care.

Each morning that week Stella laid the herbs and assessed the healing until the third day when Rufus was able to curl his fingers without pain, to hold a cup, and tie a bootlace. The scabs on the child's palm crusted dry and fell, leaving blotches of hard, dark skin mottling his hand.

"It's time now," Peter said. We sat in a ring around the daybreak fire, high on the gully crest but shielded from the winds by the river sycamores. "The child can travel, so we'll leave tomorrow early."

Stella stood from her small infirmary, wrapped the medicines into a cotton sack, and with great care, took the boy's hand. "Rufus and I will go down to the *curandero* now for his last blessing."

I leapt to my feet and declared, "I'll come with you. To say my thanks to the man and his wife for their hospitality." Already alongside her, I took her parcel and in some false and golden moment, I began to hum a jaunty tune about a world of bright and beautiful things.

Peter hesitated, leaning forward, watching us. At last he called out, "Stay here, John. I could use your help making up our road packs." But we were already half-down the hill, and my tenor voice had grown even louder with the burn of this last opportunity.

We found the woman in the doorway eyeing our descent, while the children crowded behind her peering at us.

"We'll be leaving tomorrow if the boy's hand is well enough," Stella said and led Rufus forward, lifting his arm to unwrap the linen strips.

The woman put her fingers across the top of his bare hand and pressed. "Hurt?" she asked, and Rufus shook his head. She moved his wrist joint from side to side, then turned his palm to face the sky. Suddenly she called into the house, "Adelano, *ven acá!*" The *curandero* came to the door, pushing gently through the throng of children, the smell of sweet green chiles roasting over the hearth behind them.

Kneeling on the ground before our boy, he whispered, "Show me." He took the child's hand in his, and spoke quickly to the woman in their language.

"No need for bandages," she said. "You can leave now. But the boy, he feels the earth in his blood. He is always welcome."

"This is a good boy," said the *curandero*, and put his arms around Rufus's shoulders.

"Go tell Peter that the *curandero* says you're healed," I said, and the child flew up the hill, his arms waving wildly, while I turned back to the couple. "Our pockets are empty. We left town in haste and have nothing to pay you."

"No one pays the *curandero*," said the woman.

"How do you live?" I asked, but they both turned their backs and left us in the doorway.

I began to climb the hill, reaching for Stella's hand but she leaned away from me without moving. "Come," I said to her a little too loudly. "I won't bite." I smiled, waiting.

A light autumn rain had begun, the grasses silky with the damp, and Stella said, "Now that my contract has been broken by the fire at school, I've decided to accept Peter's offer of marriage."

I had so many months to prepare for this inevitability. From the beginning any fool might have seen it, this attraction between them. Yet as eagerly as I had studied science in school, I still believed in magic, in hope; alas, in faith. I stood forlorn and defeated, thinking only of the fragrance of her body beckoning from this lonely hill. "Stella, you must reconsider. He's a decent man, but his vices will overwhelm your future." My voice was soft and lame, my stomach sick.

"What would you have me do?" she asked.

"Marry me instead! My family is wealthy. You'd never need for anything. And I'm kind, not unintelligent."

A bevy of larks rolled from a cloud, dotting the dreary charcoal sky like so many stars. Without turning to look at me, she said, "I know about your father's wealth. But that was never something I craved."

"For God's sake, Stella!" I shouted, desperation rising in my throat. "I don't understand you." The rain dripped down my face and I pushed my wet hair back from my forehead. Weakly, meekly, I said, "Just tell me what you want of me and I will become it."

"Give us your blessing," she replied. "That's all." And with that, she continued the climb up the hill to where Peter waited.

CHAPTER 20

We traveled slowly with only two horses between us. At the fork where the arroyo lay deep and dry, we halted in the cool air of the wash, the sweetwood trees scattered ahead of us down a bed of ruddy silt.

"The boy needs food," Peter said. "I expect we all do." He walked to Stella's horse where he pulled a small muslin packet from the satchel. He handed a maize cake to Rufus, shooting a quick glance at Lucy for her reaction.

"Who else?" Peter asked, and as he handed packets to the rest of us, he said to me. "You and I'll leave the others near the rail tracks before town. We'll roust in, pick up horses and supplies, then we'll all set off to deliver the girl home."

"None of us is safe in San Antonio," I replied. "Not even me."

"Not many other choices, Johnny."

"And we can't leave Rufus and the women alone while we scavenge."

"So what is your plan, then? We got no money, we're out of food. Two tired horses."

"If we can get to the telegraph office in Gonzales, I could send a message to my father for help. He never approved of my life here, but he'll send anything we need to stay alive. After all, I'm the only son left to keep his name going."

Peter laughed.

"You think I'm humorous?" I scowled.

He threw the remains of food and muslin wrapping on the ground. "I think you're callow." He lifted Rufus to the saddle again. "We need to move on."

We settled them by the river, under the autumn canopy of a smoketree and out of sight of the rail lines. Peter put a rifle in Stella's hands while I told them all to stay hidden until we returned.

"An hour in, an hour out," I said. "Just long enough to find food and horses and cash."

"But where will you go?" Stella asked. "You can't be on the streets safely."

"I have a few friends left, darling," Peter said. "Just keep that shooter ready, and we'll be back by sunset."

We rode off in the wicked spit of the wind, following the new train tracks up from Laredo, with the three left behind under the red leaves of that tree.

"We can't ride in together, Johnny," he said, "or we'll fast be noticed. You take Medina Avenue and I'll wind the backstreets. Meet me behind the Silver King."

"You think Didier and Ayla Trinka are still your friends?"

"I do. And he'll have horses and food. Fetch all the cash you can find at your boarding house and come to the alley as soon as you're able."

We trotted silently along a straight line of heavy ties and iron cross beams cut through wild thickets of winterberry. Before we reached the lumber yard, we took different paths but despite Peter's instructions, I kept to the broad corridor surrounding the rails into town.

Once at the workaday of the mill, I pulled up to watch the

clearing, waiting and measuring until passing seemed prudent. Slipping by, I rounded the curve of the rails and the crumbling adobe huts, at last into the treeless train yard opening to the sky. I intended to veer toward the liveries and away from the depot, but as I scanned the horizon of the city, I spotted a single railcar in the distance, shiny as black butter and edged with gold paint. The Pullman rested alone, a sight at once familiar and frightening, and I walked my ride slowly toward it.

At each corner stood a grim man in dark suit and low, black bowler, rifle in hand, uniformed Pinkertons, each. A buggy and driver waited ready at the bottom of the steps, and a small man waving an ivory cane stomped hard upon each while the horse jerked in fright, lowering its head and bucking its hind legs high.

Theophilus Ives, a gentleman as some called him, wore his usual tall hat and black suit, his gray mustache longer and thicker than I remembered. As he descended, he strained to grasp the crimson-painted rails of the carriage, shouting to the cabbie to control the animal.

When the man could not, my father screamed *Crop him! Crop him!* until finally the driver lifted his buggy whip and struck the horse's flanks, once, then again, and as Theophilus Ives urged him on calling *Yes! Again!* the cabbie beat the horse a dozen times more, gasping with each swing.

The horse only bucked higher and harder, and my father whirled round to face one of the Pinkertons. "Shoot it," he said, staring through the din. The chosen gunman did not hesitate but strode forward, standing firm two yards from the animal. He took a pistol from his holster and carefully pointed it at the bobbing forehead of the horse, calmly waiting for his true aim to clear.

I shouted, forcing my ride fast down the tracks toward them. The man did not flinch but took the shot, the bullet exploding between the horse's eyes. My animal pulled up hard only feet from the victim, and together we watched it tip and fall to the ground, blood seeping down its chestnut muzzle to a pool. Its face torn open, one eyeball slipped the socket and dropped free to the mud. The cabbie jumped from his rig and knelt beside the animal as it lay in the bloody weeds, its limbs twitching even in death. He leaned across its broad neck and put his cheek gently upon its mane.

My father crossed the tracks to where I sat helplessly astride my horse. "Clear the carcass," he said calmly to the others, and then turned to me. "Western horses, eh? A little more training would be useful." He pulled a small piece of lint from his wool jacket, held it between his index finger and thumb while he examined it, then disposed of it by waving his hand from side to side. "So good to see you, son."

Withdrawing a step, he crossed his arms over his chest. "Come aboard, then, boy. Come and tell me stories I can send to your ma from this Texas." He snapped the ivory cane with a flick of his wrist and tapped it on a wood crosstie at his feet. Laying his arm over my shoulder, he pulled me close, snug as a gun against the hollow of his chest, forcing me to walk with him.

He placed me on a deep satin bench opposite a glowing coal fire in the parlor of his car and rang for his servant to bring us whiskey. As a child, my father had been traded by his parents to the Vermont Ives where he labored as a field boy. He became the fastest peat cutter in all of Vermont, scrambling in the dirt for family fuel, and had explained this to me and my brother at least a hundred times. He took continual pleasure in his ironic revenge, and we sat now surrounded by the warmth of this fire, the power of his rail cars, and the carnal contentment he found in coal.

His own chair was fashioned in rich Hunter Green leather, not the largest in the room, and because of that, my father seemed bigger than he was. The hide had been recently waxed, still carrying the sickly, sweet odor of sandalwood, which, coupled with the cigar he immediately lit, caused me to become slightly nauseated.

He leaned forward across the small ebony table, spread his fingers over the gleaming black, and smiled suddenly.

"Now then, boy," he said, tracing a fingertip along the gilt trim, "where have you been these past days? I've been waiting for you since Monday last."

Without answering his question, I said in a harrowed voice, "Why are you here? You sent no word."

"I believe I still have rights to see my only son when I please." His speech was tinged with acrimony, his face wizened. I'd never seen him so; angry, of course, but never haunted by turmoil. "Expect to have the pleasure of my company more this coming year. You've likely heard we've secured our contract for the line to the City of Mexico. I'll spend some months in your grim state of Texas as we build down."

"Not here, though. Galveston, surely," I said quickly, "where your investments are."

"Son, Gould and I and the others have holdings everywhere. This Mexican contract is the newest, and it is indeed a long way from Galveston."

Exasperated, I stretched my neck back, gazing up in an effort not to react. Hand-painted hummingbirds and fuchsia blooms lay across the black ceiling, beautiful, delicate portraits that were now merely part of my own life's landscape. Stupidly, I had allowed myself to be caught in discussion when my true goal was to find money and get back to my friends. I imagined Peter waiting in the wet clay of the Silver King backyard, waiting for me to gallop in, waiting that was so unlike the man. And Stella with the others, guarded only by the cover of that tree. Caught like a fox in the coverts, I looked desperately around the carriage, perspiration seeping from my temples to my collar while my mind wheedled through ways I might escape him. "I have items to take care of today, and can't stay," I said softly, squirming pitifully.

"Your mother, poor dear, longs to hear your news, boy."

I stopped cold, straightened my back against the deep cushions, and gazed at him. My mother was never allowed to long for any of her children, not even my dead brother. I almost saw my father's words hanging in the smoky room, ancient and pointed, scrawled as though by a peasant's left hand.

"I must go," I declared, and his eyes widened. "Appointments, Father. And if you have a small sum of cash on board I could take with me...."

He walked to the whiskey bottle left by his servant and poured himself another. "I came to discuss your return to Tampico, John."

At my feet lay the preserved pelt of an African cheetah, its legs splayed by mine, its head stretched to where my father stood. I touched it lightly with the toe of my boot, suspiciously as a rat near strange bread.

"I'll not be going back to Tampico. Not ever."

"Oh, you will indeed. A question of time, only." He turned to face me, this small, frail man so carefully costumed. When he spoke, his eyes were narrow and I could not even see his thin lips beneath the mustache. "I'll have you in Mexico for some months, and then with me in Boston to shave a few heads of reprobates there."

I walked to the coach door. "Money, Father? Your help is needed today."

With a voice as sweet and decadent as a songster, he said, "I'll see you here tomorrow, John," and he stepped through the passage to the far cabin.

CHAPTER 21

"I half thought you'd left this world." Missus Cole sat on the veranda of the Villa de las Rosas, her large feet crossed at the ankles on a tiny, precarious stool. "You owe me some rents, young man." The smell of tobacco smoldered over her plum-colored wool dress, and her broad hips splayed from edge to edge of the rocker, exposing the line of her thighs under the cloth. "Three weeks' worth, Mister Ives. I'll take it now."

"Of course," I said. "The funds are in my rooms. I'll go and fetch them for you."

"There won't be any money in your rooms now." With a grand sigh she lifted her boots from the stool. "Your belongings been parceled up and moved out." Two old hens traipsed across my path, cackling at each other. "Bloody birds," she scowled and kicked them away.

"What? Why?"

"Three weeks without a word, boy! Ya coulda' been on t'a run from the law for all I know."

"I've always been a quiet and trustworthy lodger, Ma'am."

She laughed aloud and rocked back. "Have you, then?

Sodded off with nary a word for the rooms held for you or a thought for my worry? No no no no. Those rooms been cleaned an' polished, ready for a responsible gentleman. But ya still owe me for those weeks."

Thinking only of my savings, I took a deep breath. "Yes, Missus Cole. And I'll gladly settle if you'll direct me to my belongings."

"Gone," she replied. "The constable came for 'em two days ago. I hear yer father's got it all now." She slapped her lips together like a petulant child. "You didn't even inform me that the elder Mister Ives would be arrivin'. I coulda' prepared him dinner and all if I'd known."

"You let someone into my private rooms?" I asked.

"Of course. Obliged to let the law in."

"And where would I find the copper who has my items?"

"You know where to find Thomas Broc, sir. Came with two Pinkertons and said yer father sent them to fetch you." She had the skin of prunes and murky dull eyes that outstared me, outstared even her own grave. I pulled back at the thought of her and Broc touching my papers and clothes, taking my money perhaps, and only passing the remains to my father.

"Well then, Missus Cole, obviously I can't pay you until I recover my affairs."

"Figured as such, boy. I guess your father'll make me whole." She bent her head forward and as though pretending a siren, flashed her eyes up at me. In the husky voice she used for the yard mice, she hissed, "Now scat!"

Sour oak leaves lay in the mud of the alley near the Silver King. I stepped through the doorway to the barrel room, heavy with the smell of spilled whiskey and stored casks.

"Here now!" shouted Ayla Trinka. Through the dark I heard a rifle bolt slide back.

"Ayla, it's me. John Ives," I said. The muzzle of the shooter thudded softly on the floor planks.

"He's been waiting for you, John. Got himself a little irritated. Follow me now."

The darkness loosened around her shape, and we made our way toward the light where I found Peter hunched over a whitewashed kitchen worktable. A clay mug sat in front of him, copper ring stains trailing across the tabletop. At the sound of our footsteps, he looked up.

"Hell, John, where ya' been? We left the girls and the child to fend alone, man. Be dark before we get back." He waved the mug back and forth, his eyes still as a ghost's.

"I'm sorry." I sat opposite him and paused while I tried to calm my voice from the desperate dead weight of failure. "I'm afraid I've run into some bad luck."

"You want a drink, John?" Ayla asked, "Or food?"

"No, ma'am. I expect we'll be off in a stroke or two."

She smiled at me, with a kindness that shone like grace.

Peter leaned back in his chair and swept his blond hair off his taut face. "You get with some rooking young girl, Johnny?"

"No," I replied sourly. "My father has come to town. Without warning, he decided to visit me in San Antonio."

"He rolled in a week ago," Ayla said. "Least, that's what they tell me. Brought a slew a' men with 'im, gamblers and drinkers all of 'em."

"He's never come before," I said. "Even when I had malaria and couldn't see or speak."

"Oh, he's been here afore," she replied. "Coupla times I remember. Prior to your arrival, that would be."

"I don't think so, Ayla. Must've been another man's Pullman. I don't remember my father ever saying he'd traveled to Bexar. Even when I was in Tampico, he never came to visit or oversee affairs."

Peter leaped to his feet and flung the mug past my head, past the stove, crashing it against the far wall. "You have no idea what he's about, do you!" he shouted. "You think he's here just to see you?"

From the dark beyond the stove, the swing door hinges creaked, and I turned to see Didier, pistol at the ready pointing at the light. "Ayla?"

"We're fine. Just a small crockery accident."

"Well, the house is full," he replied. "We want 'em drinking and betting, not leaving because of this hullabaloo. Ayla, if you're not feeding our friends, how about a song or two for the customers?" He walked to the door and peered into the yard, his fingers arched against the wood slats like a piano man himself. "And we've got a Pink in the house now, just sat down to the monte table. Keep an eagle eye out back here fellas, and if I was you, I'd be thinkin' on leaving soon."

I saw the light glide from Peter's eyes as he looked toward the doorway. He walked to the stove, bent over it, and began collecting the broken pieces of baked clay. "How much did you bring, then, John?" he asked.

Sweating with shame, I said quietly, "Nothing. Missus Cole has evicted me. The police cleared my rooms and if I want cash from my father I'm to meet him tomorrow."

"I can't wait for tomorrow. Not safe here."

"Didier?" I asked. "Can we get a loan?"

"Sorry John. We've given all we could spare in meals and horses. But we'll hide you tonight if you stay."

"We can't risk staying the night," Peter said.

Ayla stood beside the white table, before white shelves filled with curing shanks and hocks, the flesh purpled with salt. "Haven't seen our copper today, but the Pinks asked me a few questions." Didier took her hand, lightly laying his arm across her shoulders and guiding her through the barroom door.

We waited alone in the falling daylight until we heard Ayla strike the major C chord on the piano, her very favorite because, as she had told me, it spread the harmony of hope.

"You take the supplies to Stella now," I said, "and hide out till I come, Peter. I'll go see my father in the morning on my own."

He walked out the door into the yard. I followed and found him by the hitcher rail, bridling and packing a second horse. Tussocks of high grass and autumn-yellow meadowsweet grew around him, their broken stalks mashed into the soil.

"We need that cash," I said, and he nodded without looking at me. "I'll be safe here with Ayla and Didier till I see my father tomorrow."

"I know you will. You're protected, Johnny."

"What do you mean?"

He stepped toward me, his face sharp and luminous. "Don't be ignorant. You always been sheltered by the man who pays Tom Broc. And that would be your father." His savage eyes, sad eyes, were aflame. "It was your father put Broc here. From the very beginning. Before you even fell with the malaria shakes."

At that moment, I couldn't conjure my father's face but I could hear his voice, clear and driving like water through rocks. Somewhere about my feet lay balsam roots, the smell overwhelming like chrism oil.

"Docs and criminals and coppers. Warehouse men. He owns 'em all," Peter said. "And you, for that matter."

"Not true. His interests are in Mexico, the trains and the oil. Same as Gould's."

"Theophilus Ives paid Tom Broc to come to this little nowhere town. Box a' bloody knives at the heart of it, for all I know. And you, why the hell d'ya think you ended up at the infirmary here instead of Galveston? Woulda' been easier to sail your rotting body straight there from Tampico. Christ, he had to overland you up through Apache lands to get you to San Antonio."

"I think you've lost track of your devils, Peter," I said. "My father has nothing to do with Tom Broc. Trust me."

"Broc worked your pa's docks down Galveston when the longshoremen went on strike. Then he turns up here, and soon after, you get sent to town dyin' from malaria. We see the largest disaster in memory, dozens of dead friends, buildings blown apart, and suddenly your father pitches up. The devil has come to fester right in front of us, Johnny. There's somethin' here for him, and it ain't you, boy."

I stared at him without moving. "Ridiculous," I said, and the arrogance I heard in my own voice belonged not to me but to my father.

"Men like Theophilus Ives need control more than money. And you're just the luckless lamb, waiting with your knees knocking in front of him."

"No...." I began.

"Broc went after me for an explosion he set himself. Jaime Sams knew it, and the *curandera*, too. Now they're dead. Rufus knows the truth from Lucy. We need to get free of this place so Broc can't hurt them. Or Stella."

A light rain fell in the twilight, and Peter stood alongside his horse, stroking its damp mane. He tightened the cinch strap and hoisted himself into the saddle.

"All you know are little stories. There's nothing in what you know that truly connects Broc to my father, is there?"

"We're well past the time for convincin'. Believe me or not. Up to you." He shrugged. "I should go before the Pinks find me."

Just then an amber light cast across the yard. I spun round to see Didier holding a lamp in the doorway. He watched us without speaking until Peter nodded to him, then stepped back inside the kitchen door.

"We'll wait for you till dark tomorrow, Johnny. And after, we'll be gone."

Didier offered me a secret room in the attic, behind a slatted wall lined with overflowing boxes of taxidermy. I declined, imagining riflemen on the stairs, so he moved a mat to the damp floor between the barrels in the whiskey store. There I lay while he locked and latched the alley door with an oak dropbar. I knew I shouldn't sleep that night, but all the same as the morning light hit the floor planks, I awoke to Ayla's humming.

She carried a frame with her, a painting half her size. "That Pinkerton drank so much whiskey last night, but still he won everything the depot men had, including this."

I sat up to the corridor smells of liquor and dung, staring at the image she held. A wolf pup lay alert on a satin pillow, a golden chain around its neck and a fleshy trout in its jaws. "Didn't take it with him, though."

"Firewood, then?" I asked.

"Naw. Don't ya like it? We'll hang it in the gallery. I think the colors are pretty."

I stared at her. "Colors?"

"Oh, I can see a bit. Shadows and such. The more ya hear, the more ya see, ya know."

A rider clopped into the alley and I stood quickly.

"Don't worry, John. Just the barrel man. But it's time for you to eat and leave, all the same. I put out a plate in the kitchen." The wall shook twice with thumps from the other side, and she turned her head to the sound. "And our Didier's frying up some pork." She laughed deeply, as though indulgence and mercy were the same.

"Yes," I replied. She didn't hear me, or didn't care, and remained looking toward the wall, a trace of her smile trembling still.

"Didier an' me, we never believed what the coppers said

about Olenbush." She sucked her lips hard, as though they were covered in salt. "Never believed it. An' I heard some things when Broc and Schmidt used to meet up here. Bein' blind don't mean bein' stupid."

"If you heard things that could help Peter, you'd do well to report them."

"And who would I tell, boy? Which of these coppers has your trust?"

I found Didier sitting at the kitchen table, spooning chunks of potatoes and pork to his thick lips. He tapped the plate across from him and nodded to me.

"Sit," he said.

"I think I'd better go. I should catch my father before his day starts."

"Likely more money that way, then?" He lifted his spoon, crusty purplish fingers gripping the dull wood. "They say we got near to twenty-five thousand folks in this town now, Ives. Yet the worthy ones'd fit in my barroom and still leave room for dancing. Just be careful, boy. There's a lot more smart ones than good."

I held my hand out for his, and he grasped it. "May not see you again in Bexar, but Peter and I'll find you one day," I said, and when I turned for the yard door, Ayla stood beside it, rifle in hand, staring straight ahead.

CHAPTER 22

They had packed and tethered a second horse for me, and I turned it slowly south to the depot yard, following the riverbank. As I drew close to my father's railcar, I saw the Pinkertons again, standing ready with raised rifles. Pretending to ignore them, I dismounted and walked to the steps. At the bottom was a man, tall and thin as a wren, gazing defiantly at me. He swung the barrel of his rifle to block me from the car.

"Wait there, Ives," he said, and I realized I knew him from this town, a miscreant I had last seen in Bexar County Jail, now a badged and bowler-hatted Pinkerton.

"I'm expected," I replied but he had no moment to figure his next move. From the carriage door above us came my father's voice.

"Come in, John." He presented himself in a red silk dressing gown of damask weave, uninhibited in this intimacy in front of his riflemen and track crews. I climbed the first step up and paused, staring again at his abandon, and he lifted his arm to wave me higher. "Come now, boy. There's much to discuss."

A footman unknown to me stood behind him in the

doorway, towering above my father while he stepped into the dark of the train car. I climbed quickly beyond the servant while a curlew cried through the flying dust of the yard.

The man strode around the edges of the parlor space, putting flame to wick in the corner lamps until the shadows were killed by firelight.

"Tea, sir?" he asked at last, and my father nodded.

Heartily, I added, "I will have coffee," and in some deep place, some cave of childhood, I believed that this demand would prove my manhood.

"Now, I'm willing to put money in your hands today, but you must be willing to make commitments first."

Of course he harbored requests in exchange. No act of Theophilus Ives was ever free of brokerage. He lifted a page from the small table at his knee, and pushed it at me, my grandfather's heavy gold Masonic ring, a diamond surrounded by a large carved compass and skull, on his index finger.

Before I could respond I heard soft steps, slippers perhaps, wandering down the passage behind him. I looked up to see a woman, standing in the light of the doorway, and my father snapped his head round to look as well.

She smiled, her small bow-shaped mouth already deep red with rouge. "Your son, Theo?" she asked. She wore only a dressing gown herself, of pale pink silk, cloth so thin, I could perceive her hips and calves as she moved.

I looked to my father. I had only ever heard my uncle and my mother call him by this shortened name.

"Yes, Nora," he replied, wholly without modesty in front of me. "This is John."

Standing from my chair, I held my hand to her. Without clasping it, she scraped her fingernails across my outstretched palm, hovering like over dead prey.

"Nora Nesbit," she said, her blue eyes wide though sadly shadowed.

"I expect you've heard of her from New York or London," added my father. I hadn't, but saying this would not have aided my financial situation, so I nodded quietly. "Noted by the critics for *Penzance,* and *Pinafore,* too." He put a hand on her shoulder and glanced at his empty teacup. "Do see to the man, Nora. He's meant to be bringing our morning meal." Instead of obeying, she sat beside him on the velvet bench, her pinkish fingers resting on the folds of his gown.

Her ankles were revealed below the hem of her silk, the skin so thin and white, so fragile she might never have encountered daylight. Her hair, glossy blonde curls, thick and wild, fell across her shoulders. She pushed the wisps from her face, and her skin was already heavily dusted with porcelain powder. She took a cigarette from an ivory box on the table and turned to my father without speaking, waiting for him to put a light to it.

"Theo tells me you've been convalescing here for some time." She spoke softly, and her mouth barely moved as she did, but her voice was husky with the childish propriety of an English actress. She smiled, and my father struck a match to her Benson.

"I was," I replied, "but no longer. I've been working on the *Light* in town. Reporting."

"I love a man clever with words," she said. "Don't I, Theo?"

My father did something then I'd never seen him do before: he grinned, broadly and unabashedly.

She began to speak again, but suddenly I snapped at her, "How old are you?"

"Don't be rude, boy. The age of a woman is never your affair," my father said.

"Do you even know how old I am?" I asked her. "I'll happily disclose it. I'll be twenty-seven in the coming year."

"Which makes you twenty-six at the moment," she said, attempting sarcasm. Indeed, my father smirked at her joke.

"Are you even as old as I am?"

"No," she replied, and then softly, "Successful stage actresses are often young. It's really of no matter." Her cheeks flushed beneath the white powder, as though her supreme truth had been uncovered.

My father's gentleman appeared in the doorway holding a large tray. "Sir?"

"Place it here," my father said, "and clear the rest to my desk." He was abrupt and irritated, a change so sudden from his demeanor with Nora Nesbit. "No, no, bring that top paper back." He held his hand out, looking not at the servant but at me, and handed the page to me again. "Did you bring coffee? Pour the boy his coffee then while he reads."

"I need to see a dressmaker today," Nora said, and touched the fold of red silk on his shoulder. "How much longer did you say we will be in San Antonio, Theo?"

"Quiet. Let him read." But instead, he pulled the page from my fingers and barked, "You were always so slow at your studies!" Leaning toward me, he said, "It's straightforward. You sign this agreement and I will deposit a year's wages in your name with Brackenridge's bank. Follow the commitments listed and the money is yours, in addition to any past salary for your employment at the Mexican Central Railroad."

"You can stop there. I'm not going back to Mexico."

"Then I can't help you, boy. According to our agreement..."

"We have no agreement."

"...according to our agreement, which you will sign, you must meet me in Tampico on the tenth of February, sixty days from now. I'll not require you home for Christmas this year, but you'll come to Tampico where you will learn a trade more complex than merely handing pay packets to drunk laborers. By

June, you'll be in Boston. Gould has agreed a place for you in the company."

A small vitrine of mementos from his travels sat alongside the bench, displaying several blue jade warhorses carved in South America, a knife with florid silver scabbard, a pistol the color of wine, all objects he had collected, and prized, for years. He lifted his fingers from Nora's gown and laid them on the case, idly caressing it as well.

"Sign it," he said. "You don't really have to read the details, boy. You're my son, after all."

The dull morning moon lingered like smoke over the yard where dry fields of cattle bordered our tracks. Homely howls of railmen and cowpokes drifted through the clerestories, and my father, lodging himself between it all, held the contract and his gold pen out to me. "Sign it."

Nora Nesbit looked first at me and then at my father. With her hand gently cupping his shoulder, she whispered, "You're such a bully, Theo." She giggled faintly as a child might.

He turned suddenly to scrutinize her, and Nora's amused expression altered, her blue eyes widening, her lips dropping slightly open.

He put the pen on the table and drew his arm back, his fingers clenched. She shifted slightly away, but he was too quick. With a dark stare, he unleashed his fist, swift and hard across her face, the sound of bone cracking where that ring struck.

"Father!" I shouted.

She cried out and covered her powdered face with her hands, the blood smearing pink across her cheeks. She rose and ran from the room, and he watched her, shaking his head.

"Learn this, boy, if you learn nothing else. However precious they may be, women have only one place in this world." He took her burning cigarette from the ashtray and stabbed it out.

"Nothing gives you license to do such a thing," I whispered, bowing my head, afraid, always afraid, to look him straight.

"Oh, but there are one or two things," he muttered, and I lifted my gaze. His mouth had crooked into a half-smile, his lips drawn tight to the color of pus.

"Her nose may be broken, and she certainly needs a doctor!" I grabbed the page from the vitrine and crumpled it in my fist. Walking to the carriage door, I turned to him once more and asked, "Was this how you brought Daniel to his death?"

I opened the door and stood in the fresh air as he said, "Sign the damn paper or not. It's your decision, John."

"Of course you're a bully. You always were." I strode past him, through the carriage beyond the parlor, and into his private rooms.

Nora sat at a small vanity, watching herself in a mirror. She held a handkerchief to the bridge of her nose, dabbing and rinsing it of the blood in a bowl at her elbows. As I drew closer, the soft scent of eglantine roses lifted from her shoulders.

"Let me see, please. I've some experience with this kind of break."

She looked at my reflection, nodded, and removed the cloth from her face. The blue of her irises had paled to the color of linnet eggs, and her cheeks glowed red with blood. A gash, open and seeping, extended from the bridge bone across her lower eye socket. Her entire face had begun to swell.

"I believe it's broken. You'll need someone to see to it."

"Damn ring of his," she said. "He put it on for you to see."

A shadow crossed the doorway and I turned to see my father's servant. "Mister Ives has requested that you leave," he said to me. He didn't stand firm, but shifted from left foot to right.

"Come, Nora," I said. "Dress yourself quickly and I'll take you to the surgery."

"No," she replied. "This isn't the first time." She put the cloth back across her nose to stay the blood, and then gazed at me full-on, and her face, once a bright, three-pointed star, was now a swollen mash, creased into purpling, lumps of flesh.

"Your clothes," I said. I walked to my father's man. "I'm taking Miss Nesbit to the infirmary."

His skin was gray as stone, and his eyes tilted down at the corners as he looked at her.

"I told you no, John," Nora said. "Now please get out of my rooms. You are only causing a worse situation by staying."

She pulled a large pot of greasepaint from the table and began dipping the blood-soiled kerchief into it. She smeared the white paste over her cheeks, over the blood and the bone and the wound, grimacing as she did.

The servant moved forward, blocking Nora from my view. "You must go," he said, his voice deep and gentle like a bear just rising from winter. "There's nothing more for you to do here."

"Nora?" I said again. When she didn't answer me, I turned away and walked through the empty parlor into the daylight and the silence.

CHAPTER 23

I followed the line of winterberry trees near the rails south of town, and reaching the river, I slipped from my horse to drink. Rain had pooled near the edge of the riverbank, and those silky waters tasted of stone and leaves. Scattered around me in the shimmering mud were fallen berries, the colors of flame and poison. I slumped to the ground and stared at the sunlight streaming through the trees until I no longer could, until between me and the sun remained only the membrane of dreams.

I woke at dusk. Still a city child, I had slept far too long, naïve and vulnerable beside the frontier road. I hurried to my feet only to find Peter a few yards away, kneeling at the water's edge. He dipped his hat and filled its crown without speaking to me.

"Couldn't keep my eyes open anymore," I said and walked to him. "Coming to find me?"

"I'd like to answer yes, Johnny." He flung what remained of the water back into the river. Standing on the cold, dark shore, he watched an egret rise to flight, gliding through the wind like a knife. "But no, I've been hunting for Lucy. She ran off hours ago."

"Isn't she on foot?" I asked. "Should be easy to find her."

He pushed his blond hair, matted and unwashed, back off his broad forehead, and squinted at me as though in pain.

"Are you injured?" I asked.

"No. Just need to find the girl and get back to Stella."

"I expect Lucy doesn't want to be found."

"Not sayin' she does. I'm sayin' that's the job before us." He dropped the hat to the bank and stared at me, his brow heavy above those dark green eyes. Pursing his lips, he said, "I'll ride down the river edge again. You helpin?"

"Of course."

"Then cross to the woods on the other side. She'll likely be hidin' in those trees if she made it over."

I took my mare through the sodden switchgrass and into the shallows. We waded in the sand with no lantern to guide us while she hoofed deftly between the stones. Coming up the far bank into a stand of sycamore and cypress, we rode for an hour between the trees and the fields shining with the new rain and the moon.

I heard Peter's voice calling me back like a death angel, and I crossed the Medina again, half expecting the girl's body to appear in the riverflow.

"I been huntin' for hours," Peter said. "She could be hiding, or even drowned." He dropped his reins and squeezed his palms hard over the pommel. "But if we don't find her tonight, we'll lose her to the wolves or the river or the cold. That's certain. No weapon, no food, mad to her bones. Girl like her could never survive this place."

"Stella and Rufus are also alone," I said, and he nodded, his long blue shadow wavering in the last of the moonlight. "Panther can find them just as easily."

He gazed at me, sullied lips parted.

"Come on, Peter. Better the living. No sense keeping on for that girl. She doesn't even want us."

"Not doin' this for her. I'm doin' it for Stella, to keep her heart from breaking."

I nodded, but all the same, I pressed my right leg to the horse's flank, easing my left rein out, turning onto the trail toward camp. Peter turned as well and followed. The sudden weight of our decision lit the center of every pore of my skin. Someone had cut Lucy's mother cord at birth, wiped her dry and clean, and after all that effort, on this day, Peter and I turned back and left her.

As we rode toward the smoketree and the culvert, we watched one another without speaking. We found Stella propped against the trunk, her face obscured by a large branch of thick leaves. Rufus slept on the bluestem grasses beside her. She held his harmed hand in hers, and it was dark with scars that would never disappear under anyone's holy ministering.

Stella turned slowly to our sound without speaking, a small figure hiding close to the earth. She moved her fingers roughly across the mash of rotting autumn beneath her legs.

As we drew closer, she stood from under the tree. Her gray eyes were small and tense, and down the center of her face lay a ribbon of darkness.

"You couldn't find her?"

Peter stepped toward her, held his hands out, but she didn't move. Her cheeks were damp, and her skin glittered like fire.

"No," he replied.

"Come and sit," she said and walked to a neat stack of tinder and kindling she had gathered. "You can go out again after you eat and drink. It'll be easier to find her now the two of you are working at it together."

"We've been everywhere we could." His voice was low and

wretched. "Behind every tree, over the river. She's not to be found, Stella."

"My God, she's running from us! Of course it's not easy." Suddenly, she strode to my horse and began removing its packs, throwing them to the grasses until she'd relieved the animal of the weight. "It's my fault she got away. She set out for the river and I didn't even think to follow her. She seemed so peaceful. These hours with us, she almost found her true self again." She hoisted herself into the saddle, pulling her skirts up and sitting astride, restless and wild.

"Most likely she'll be back on her bedroll by dawn. In fact," I lied, "it's a common fallacy that those who wander need to be sought, that they won't return home. Usually they do."

"I can't let my sister die out here, even if you can."

"We'll be losin' the moonlight soon," Peter said. "We can't hunt her in the dark." He took Stella's reins in his fist, thumbing the soft leather while he spoke. "This'll be hard for you to hear, love, but she might have drowned if she tried to cross the Medina." The scream of a hunting owl fell through the low clouds, and Peter put his hand on Stella's leg, touching her exposed flesh. He moved to lift her down, but she bristled away from him.

"Don't," she said. "If it's a body we'll find, then we need to find it. My mother has the right to know what happened to her child." But Peter pulled her gently from the saddle and she slipped down this time without protest. She stared into the thick vegetation behind us, and slowly, carefully, stepped back into its shelter. She knelt in the cool mud, the lurid smell of softened, rotting tissue somewhere near.

Rufus sat up and she rested her palm on his small shoulder. She put her lips to his forehead and whispered gently, "I'm sorry we woke you, child."

"Miss?" he asked, staring at her fevered face.

Stella pulled him to her side. "I'm fine, sweetheart. Look, John's back and we'll be going to our new lives soon."

I took the water jug from where she'd tossed it beside the horse, and filled a deep blue cup for her. "Here. You need to drink."

"Give it to Rufus first. His throat will be dry from sleep."

The boy looked up at me with his chary face but reached for the cup. He emptied it and asked for more, and I filled it again with the dark, sweet water.

"Some supper and then sleep," Peter said. "I'll search again at dawn. Johnny'll come, too. Won't you?"

"Yes," I said and walked to where Stella had begun to lay the stone circle and branches. "Let's get this fire up. You cold, Rufus?"

The child nodded but watched Stella.

"I'm sorry, son. I wasn't thinking," she said, crouching as she tucked her blanket around him. "Of course you're chilly."

And in this night of hunger and failure, of the moon escaping us, the boy opened his eyes wide and smiled at her. "Thank you, Mama," he said, in a voice soft like a little river, and for a moment I forgot I had just left a girl for dead.

Peter and I stood alone on the Medina crest where a dawn snow had speckled the landscape. "I think she must've drowned," he said, watching those white flowers melt into the river. "She wasn't strong enough or fast enough to get clear of us. I bet the current carried her away."

I teetered on a large rock, black and slippery under my boot leather, feeling the sudden icy kick of the winds off the water. "We can't keep on like this, giving Stella an inch of hope while we ride in circles."

"What would you have me do? Tell her the truth?"

I snapped my head to glare at him. "There's no truth to tell. Neither of us knows where that girl is now. Just another frontier child disappeared. Maybe drowned, maybe one year someone'll find her alive somewhere."

Crying birds rounded like small, blackened angels through the clouds, and bits of snow clung beside us on the grasses. "I want to try again to find her," he muttered. "For Stella's sake."

A starveling of love for so long, I was utterly unused to it. I'd always remember that look on his face, his bent, dark head staring oddly at me, as though for approval.

"You can't make this right," I said. "When I saw Lucy in the cave she was already prey, already at her end." A single sycamore stood behind him, and through the lines of its crooked branches, the purple dawn was spreading against the black. "Look, I'll tell Stella if you want. Here's the only truth she needs to hear. Alive or dead, her sister can't be saved. *Curandero* was right. Might as well cut off this search now."

"I'd never allow you to tell her that!" His skin was gray as stone. "You got no soul anymore, Johnny. Know that?"

I didn't know if the sun would rise that day or if the sky would hang dark and low till night. I didn't know much of what had happened to him in his difficult life, nor he in mine. All I knew was that he had been my friend and though I'd lost her to him, still that was true.

"I'm sorry," I said.

He brought his hands together and rubbed them hard against the cold. Nothing glittering lay on him, nothing miraculous, but even with his brow thick and eyes nearly closed, I believe he tried to smile.

Standing at last before the boy and Stella, Peter was faithful to his word. He stepped forward across the snow-spotted thistles and took her hand, walking her through the brush, away from us. He hunched over exhausted. She held a cloth in her hands, folding it and unfolding it as she watched him speak. Once she turned to our camp and I saw her nod. Eventually he raised his hand and wiped two fingertips across her cheek. That's when I saw him lift her chin for a kiss. I watched them until my throat tasted of fire, and then I turned away because they had healed together, now indistinguishable.

"Rufus!" she called out, waving. The boy ran to her, and she knelt to embrace him. Together, the three crossed the cold field and stood with me.

Peter hesitated to speak until Rufus could not wait any longer. "Mister Ives! We're all going to California! You comin' with us?"

"Well, well," I said, my voice paced and deep like my father's. "I'll think on it."

"Swear you will?"

"Of course, boy. It's an enticing invitation." Looking past him to Stella and Peter, I added, "An invitation from all of you?"

"Yes," she said.

"And when are you planning to leave?"

"We'll check the trains, be collecting some debts, our personals," Peter replied. "Soon as we're able."

"Heading to town again?" I backed against the frozen bark of the tree trunk, and began to roll my bedmat. A damp web hung along the lowest branch, and half-blind with weariness, I struck at it. Frail as air in that cold morning, I was now running short of wherewithal.

"Gotta be careful, to be sure," Peter said. "But there's no way around it. We plan on leavin' Rufus at the Silver King while we attend to things."

"Leave the boy? Don't be ridiculous. Look, I've nothing left to collect. I'll stay at the King with them until you're set to go."

I thought of that girl who had come to read to me before we

entered the maze of this far earth, of the town that had brought me hard luck, of my father who planted me here for nothing more than his own medieval vanity. I packed my saddle bag and slipped my gun into its holster, my rifle into its scabbard.

"Come on. Maybe I'm not ready for California, but certainly I can be of use one more time in this ghastly place."

CHAPTER 24

The light was up but not the sun by the time we neared the fork of San Pedro. With Peter and the others far behind, I'd come through the woods imagining myself alone, but reaching the river I heard music, and I slipped from my mount to the ground to peer through the tree cover. Before me lay a meadow carpeted with ponyfoot vine, inhabited by a dozen wagons and their inhabitants. The noise of the animal corrals provided cover, and I held my breath, listening to these people, all of them raucous and armed.

The women trudged to the creek and back as they filled buckets with water, dumping it into a large iron pot at their camp. Along the muddy bank waited four men in ill-fitting, worn suits, squatting on their haunches. One stood and walked to the pot, setting the wood underneath it alight. Under his soiled dark clothing, he wore a clean white shirt, cuffs drooping over his wrists and a collar sitting high on his neck.

Two fiddlers strutted back and forth at the waterside, their melody faint and playful. These old fellows, grinning and wild, stopped walking when they reached the women but continued to play louder and louder. One of the younger men stood and waved his revolver at them, shouting something in a language I didn't understand. The musicians continued striking bow to strings through the cold morning air while the members of this tiny society gathered round the iron pot tossing living frogs into the water. Once they had emptied their pockets and aprons, they stood back and watched the boil, listening to the hissing of burning skin.

By then the fiddlers had laid down their violins and walked to the far wagons. When they returned, they came with a woman dressed in a red shift, and even at that distance I knew it was Lucy. They brought her to the creek, and she came meekly without complaint, her bad leg dragging through the weeds.

"Ulka!" one of them called out, looking at her. "Ulka," he said again, and put his arm around her gaunt shoulders. As he did, she pressed forward, straining against the men to draw closer to the pot, breathing the steam as it rose.

"Lucy!" I called and swung myself onto the mare, but my voice was too small and not even the children turned to me. "Stop! Stop there!" I shouted and trotted from the shelter of the trees into the meadow.

They allowed it, these families who lived on the edge of loss; they turned and lifted guns, to be sure, but permitted me to weave through them until I neared the girl.

"These fields were swollen in the night," she said, crouching closer to the boil. "More'n I thought possible. Even the rabbits're shiverin'."

The dawnlight sharpened our shadows, and she tried to push the men off until they released her and moved away, shaking their heads.

"Have you been kidnapped?" I whispered, taking her mud-smudged hand.

"No," she said, and shook her head hard, looking about as though to escape me.

One of the men stepped back to us and handed her a white, woolen shawl. "She'll be cold standin' so far from ta' boil."

"Why do you hold her?" I asked.

"What d'ya mean, fella?" He rubbed his hand over his nose. "No one keepin' this girl with us. Came here as a shooter star. Asked to stay." His skin was grimy and crusted with narrow scabs. His clothes, a black mismatched jacket and trousers, were shiny from days of soil. "She yer kin?"

"No. Well, yes, sort of." I took the shawl from her hands and wrapped it round her. "I'm here to take her home. To protect her."

"Fine job ya done so far," he said, and chuckled slyly. To the left of us nearer the woods the corral of horses fluttered, then snorted, and when I looked, all of them were pawing through piles of pine needles. He shifted to watch, then lifted his rifle. "Over to, boys! Watch 'em! Summun's comin' to take 'em!"

"No, it's only the girl's family," I said. "They don't want your horses."

Peter appeared from beneath the low-hanging willow branches, leaning forward in his saddle and ducking across the horse's neck. He held a cocked Colt at his hip, but moved judiciously toward us while the families stepped aside to allow his passing.

"Give me your hand, Lucy," he said leaning over to lift her.

"Why?" she asked.

"Because we're going to take you home."

"Where's my sister?"

I snapped my head round to stare at her. "Your sister?" I asked. "You remember Stella now?"

She nodded silently.

"Hiding in the woods," Peter said. "I left them in a safe place."

"Kindly ones here," Lucy replied. "Safe here. Said I could

stay with 'em but I need to give my sister something first. Where is she?"

One of the men stepped up to Peter. "If you be kin of ta girl, you may take 'er. But only if she's willin'. She been tellin' us some tales, 'n' we can see she been bad held by folks." The man looked to the ground where the grasses rose around us, thick and clean and shining like the river. "We be eatin' our meal now," he said, "and you can partake. Go bring yer other kin for *hobben*."

Peter looked across the meadow to the families, across to their men, who were still armed even as they grabbed their bowls.

"We ain't yer enemy," said the man. "You be the reckless ones comin' through our peace."

Peter nodded to me. "Go fetch Stella and Rufus," he said, and I mounted my mare again. I trotted past the children standing beside tangled blackberry vines, nothing for them to pluck in this cold season and the low horizon like a scratchy heaven.

"Ai there!" they called, waving and laughing at me as I rode on for my family while the thin light spread through the eastern sky.

On our return, Stella, the child, and I all rode slowly from under the cover of low-hanging willow branches. As we approached Lucy, dressed in red and wrapped in white wool, she was beautiful as I'd never understood. I saw the sleepy curiosity deep in her eyes, heard her silky breath in the chilled river wind, and even that hideous smile struck wonder.

I pulled my horse up as we neared, and Stella jumped down. It had begun to rain, and she stumbled in the marsh, pushing herself back to stand and running until she wrapped herself round the bony barrel of Lucy's body.

"I worried so!" she exclaimed. "We thought you might've drowned!"

Lucy kissed her and nodded. "I'm not harmed. And look, I found some good folk to be my family."

The marsh people gave us bowls of hot broth and we sat cross-legged by the fire on a bright green blanket. One of the fiddlers offered his jacket to Lucy, who allowed him to drape it over her shoulders.

"We've come to take you home," Stella said. "Where you'll be safe."

Lucy gazed hard at her. "This's my home now." She watched a procession at her feet, a parade of ants winding through the ponyfoot. Crushing a knot of them between her fingers, she brought the nugget to her lips and began to chew.

"These people are voyagers," Stella replied. "You stay with them and I'll never see you again. They'll keep you moving, working hard, maybe even leaving Texas."

"I do need to leave Texas before that devil Tom Broc gets to me again. The Lord sees we can't go back to San Antonio." She pointed plain and hard at Peter. "And *you* know. Rufus knows, too. Jaime told us all what they had in Schmidt's stores. Boxes and boxes of ledger sheets that can stop every train in our world. Broc ordered Jaime to set them all to fire." She stooped and filled her fists with mud. "And then burned him alive for knowing."

She began to cry so quietly, and the men drew closer, encircling her.

"*He's* known all of it," she nodded at Peter. "He's got some secrets. They both do!" She walked to where I sat, standing over me, stiff and wild. "You never tell your secrets, do you?"

Stella turned to Peter, not angry but weary, a stone rubbed too long against the world. "What does she mean?" she asked.

He held his hands to her cheeks. "Broc's been hiding company books in that warehouse for months, records of the rail business into Tampico. He was ordered to set that fire and get rid of 'em once and for all. And after he killed Jaime, he went to the

Sams house to kill the rest so there'd be no one alive who knew. But he found Lucy there, too. *Curandera*'d been keepin' her. He'd tried to kill your sister once in his own rage, and when he found her that night with the Sams family, he went at her."

Lucy didn't edge from this lamentation, didn't move. The sound of the wind rose, bringing with it a cluster of small birds, glistening in the rain, and the girl's crooked face crinkled at the sight.

"She healed me, poor woman," she said calmly, not afraid anymore.

Peter took a deep breath, and again. Over and over, he sucked the cold wind into his lungs, then looked at Stella without moving closer, his gaze unbreakable.

"But I was there. Lucy called it a gift from God tho' I never been called that before or since. Broc broke the door off and shot at the *curandera*. Two times, till she fell and her black hair lay in her own blood." Peter drew his hands back and reached into an inner pocket, pulling from it a curved knife. "He tried to get to Lucy with this," he whispered. "But he never had a talent for cutters. I got your sister and Rufe free, and left the man with a gouge of his own knife that he won't soon forget."

Lucy stood and moved along the shallows away from us.

"Broc is a killer," Peter said, "and he works at the pleasure of other murderers. Eh, Johnny? Your father's got plenty invested in the Boston & Galveston."

Lucy continued walking, faster now, pulling the wild lilies and yawning as she went like a dog under threat. When she reached the woods she stopped, and turned abruptly to face us. "Been looking for family my whole life," she said. "Found these at last." She lifted a large, broken bough from where it lay in the mud and dug it back into the ground with hammering strength. "They want me with 'em. They've been kind to me and I'll be staying on."

Cold and dreamless, I walked away and called over my shoulder. "We need to leave this place, this town and river and all of its people." I mounted my horse. "Come or not, Lucy." I shrugged.

"I can't leave without her," Stella said. She went to her sister and put her hand out to touch the dry, pale skin of Lucy's emaciated arm.

The girl smiled at her, and slipped a hand into the pocket of her shift, drawing from it a large black coin.

"What's this?" Stella asked.

"Maybe you remember that young preacher who carved coal when we lived at home. He came to our farm and gave me this." Lucy held out her hand and offered the gift to Stella.

"Oh, my darling." Stella gazed at it, perplexed, and as she did, she began to cry.

"It's for you." Lucy put her hand to Stella's face. "Please don't cry," she said. "I didn't want to make you sad. He gave me it out of love, and now I give it to you the same way. Look, he carved my name here, and a heart."

Peter strode to the two women, standing close but not close enough to touch, hovering only as a guard might.

"Sister," Stella whispered. "Do you remember that man? You were seventeen that year."

"Just that he lived in the broken barn for a time before he died."

"You don't remember that man was your husband?" Stella asked. She bent forward, leaning against Peter while he put his arms helplessly around her. "Don't you want to see our home again? Your family?"

Lucy rubbed her eyes hard; round and round she scratched her fingers across the disfigured side of her face. "I made you sad. I'm sorry," she said. "Wouldn't hurt you for the world." She pulled a hemp string from her pocket and handed it to Stella.

"This can be your wedding locket, sweet child." She waited then, and the gray day was so quiet I thought for a moment I heard the creek moving over the river pebbles. "I can't go back to town, but you go fetch what you need and come back for me. I promise I'll go home with you, sister, to see you married. We always woke so early there. D'you remember?"

CHAPTER 25

By the time we reached San Fernando Church the steeples were mottled with dying shadows and on the plaza, the chili queens had already begun serving supper to the crowds. We turned quickly down Dolorosa, a quiet dirt road leading to the west edge of town. Rounding the alley behind the Silver King, we brought our horses into the yard and found Didier bending over the trough, water dripping from thick, dark bags under his tiny eyes. In that moment he saw us, he didn't appear much of a frontier man, gray hair and brows, skin lined with creases like used leather. Stunned at our arrival, he moved as though in pain, staring, then settling, and finally smiling at us like a poised fellow pulling lightning from the sky.

"And here I am minding my own affairs," he called. "Didn't expect to see you again, my friends." He extended his hand with a welcome, rough and sweet at once. "Best get inside, though." He lifted Rufus onto his shoulders. "Good to see you, boy. Learn anything from this salamagundi gang? Lemme see that hand now." Rufus held his deformed hand low so Didier could examine it.

"The burns have healed," Stella said. "And he's able to use it."

Didier nodded, then ducked himself and the boy through the doorway. "Come now," he repeated. "Quick."

The kitchen was lit, but the other rooms were silent. Ayla sat in a chair by the stove, a glass of whiskey on the table before her. Didier crossed to her and took the glass, gulping it empty, then rested his hand on her shoulder.

"Where're your customers?" Peter asked.

"We're closed. Broc shut us down," Ayla said.

"What reason?"

She hesitated. "He didn't need a reason, now did he?" A small rat moved across the floor and Ayla cocked her head at the sound of its scratches. Lifting her small boots off the planks, she waited for it to pass. "All he needed was a couple of Pinkertons to board up the front."

"Was this because of my sister?" Stella asked. "Did my family bring this on you?"

The whistle and bang of the evening train plowed through the air, and we fell to quiet. A faint patter of rain began, leaving the musty smell of limp flowers seeping inside the open back door.

Ayla walked to it, closing and latching it. "No, ma'am," she answered. "The copper accused us of egging on the crimes of this town in our saloon."

"Meaning," Didier added, "his Pinks were here and killed a couple cattlemen in the bar. Whenever Broc makes an accusation, you can be sure he's giving away his own guilt." Two green glass bottles sat on the chipped white paint, and he grabbed these in one arm. "Come out front. I'd be delighted to pour for you all."

He took Ayla's hand and guided her through the door, and as we followed, he lifted Rufus to sit on the counter. He limped behind the bar then, those pale bones, hollow bones, carrying his dreams. He pulled whiskey and lemonade from the shelf. Behind him on the wall hung the life-size portrait of the yellow-eyed wolf pup, that dying fish in its teeth.

Rufus gazed up at it, gulping, his bad hand snapping to cover his mouth. The child reached into his pocket and pulled a cluster of rosemary, holding it to his face while he peeked at the iridescent silk of the dying fish.

Didier bent, arms encircling him. Softly, he said, "It's only a picture, boy. Not a real wolf."

Rufus nodded slowly, still staring at the painting. The boards over the window glass were hammered tight, and only light from the lanterns lay across the room. "Can I get down?" he asked. Peter lifted him to the floor, and the child wiped his hands on his pantlegs. "Do you smell some blood?"

"No," Didier replied. "The room has been closed up for days, that's all. Bad air." Turning to Peter, he mumbled, "Where is the mad girl?"

"With the marsh people down by the river fork south of town. She was afraid to come back here with us. We'll be gathering our affairs now from our rooms, fetch her, and then get a train up to Rockdale to the Moore family's ranch. Though we gotta find some cash money for the tickets."

Didier pushed his sleeves up his forearms, the loose skin slacking across his elbows. Lodged under the wool at the hinge of his bones was a pocket derringer, the nose of German silver gleaming against the flame. He pulled it free and laid it on the bar counter. "I'd give you more if I had it," he said. "Being closed down like this, well, we're using everything we saved."

"I understand," Peter said, and took his own weapons from their sheaths, setting them on the glossy bar. "I'm at fault for what's happened to us; I bungled the work of this life." And like a dog in the twilight, he bent forward and stretched his neck and arms on the counter oak. "It's to me, just me, to repair it."

I did nothing, said nothing; watched him only. A gentleman, no; a man running in pain and about to burn like a moth.

Didier turned from him to the darkened public doors. He flexed a sallow-skinned muscle, old and soft. "You don't want to be moving in town in such a big group," he said. "Even after dark, people notice threes and fours more than twos."

"We'll be fine, fine."

"We'd do better leaving the boy here," I said.

Didier waved an arm at Peter, and the slope of white fat ringing his neck quivered as he did. "I'm tellin' ya' a truth, here Olenbush. Don't be an arrogant ass with the lives of your girl and your child. Leave them with me while you move about."

"I'm completely capable of making my way safely across town," Stella said. "Just give me something to shoot with. I was raised to it."

Peter put a rough hand across hers, covering it. "Of course," he murmured. "The two of us will go. Johnny, you'll stay here to keep watch? Three doors is too many for one man to cover, eh Didier?"

"To be sure," I said. "I have nothing left in this town to collect."

"You understand, Rufus?" Stella reached to touch the boy's small, sleek head and he turned his face to hers. "You'll stay here with Ayla and Didier, and John as well. Peter and I will be back in an hour or so. You must be very good while we're gone."

"Y'all can sleep here tonight," Ayla said. "I'll sort the beds for you."

Didier began to walk to her, but as he rounded the bar, he stopped suddenly. "Goddamn it," he muttered. He stepped forward and put all his weight on the right leg. "Damn cramps."

I dragged a chair to him. "Here, sit down for a moment."

He nodded without looking at me. "Merci, sir." Slumping over his knees, he breathed hard. "The Pinks're watching us night and day. You would do better to get out of the city before the morning. Broc has an army of those criminals to hand and they're just waitin' for Olenbush to show himself." He nodded toward the boy. "For anyone with secrets."

Peter lifted his guns from the bar. He handed one to Stella, and walked to the back door, peering through the crack. "Yard's empty. Let's go."

Stella knelt beside Rufus and kissed his forehead. "See you in a little while," she said smiling, and ran to the back door.

They had been gone only a few moments when I heard footsteps creaking on the boardwalk at the front. Didier nodded to me and went to extinguish the lamps in the barroom. I followed him and waited near the front doors, staring through the gaps into the darkness. The steps faded, lumbering slowly toward the church, and I saw the shadow of a man at the far corner, pausing in the thin lamplight. I turned to Didier, but he had moved back into the kitchen. My heart in my fist, I scurried after him.

"You need to get Rufus somewhere safe," I said. "People are out there and I can't tell the drunks from the Pinks."

I listened and watched a moment more, holding my revolver tight and low until suddenly thuds of flesh struck the saloon front boards.

"Probably just an angry patron," Didier said. "We're the last call for 'em. Keep quiet and they'll go away." The stove fire cast a red glow through the mica glass, and the smell of cedar char lay across the dark, smoky room. Didier touched his hand, nails black from soot, to the derringer now lodged in his waistband. "Since they closed me we had a coupla fellas. Drunks leaving the Elephant looking for a jigger," he whispered.

"More likely Pinkertons," I said. "Is your alley door locked?"

"Always," Ayla said. "I put the latch down myself."

"Stay here." I slipped my forty-five into its holster, and took my rifle from the table.

I lifted the lever and chambered a round, then stepped quietly down the dank hall to the side door. The barrel ricks were full, the damp sod reeking of rancid tobacco. I waited in the dark, listening for movement on the other side of the door. Finally, I lifted the heavy latch. Silver light streaked the passageway as I pressed on the door and peered into the alley. With neither movement nor human echo beyond me, I took a step forward.

A man moved into the streetlight from behind the door, a huge, grizzled fellow with big-knuckled hands. He lurched forward and I backed against the doorway, raising the rifle without firing. He swung a powerful right. I leaned away, moving out of his range then shifted back and braced myself against the jamb.

Putting my rifle again to eye level, I aimed for flesh, for the bulk of him, if only to stop his next move on me. I squeezed and barely saw the flicker of light before the sound exploded.

The burning smell of powder filled the sudden silence and I froze, not even sure the bullet had made contact until I saw blood on his thigh. He slumped to the side and grabbed his leg, while I lifted the butt of the rifle and brought it down on his jaw, then his shoulder, slamming the gun against bone until he lay unconscious in the winter mud.

I charged past the black pit of the taproom. Stopping at the edge of the kitchen, the sudden light across the floor like fire, I saw Didier and Ayla hovering beside the back door.

Deep shouts came from the yard, and a shot struck the latch from close range, the iron and oak sparking gold.

"Get out of the doorline, for God's sake!" I said, pointing my Colt at the fragile center of the door. I pulled the trigger and my bullet penetrated the wood clear through. A heavy weight thudded against the door.

In the few seconds of silence that followed, Didier blew the lamps and the room grew black.

"Open now!" called a voice suddenly, and the sound of shuffling feet came from the yard.

"Take the boy out the side door," I whispered.

A loud crash slammed the door, and then another as the wood splintered with the blow of a heavy boot.

"Go!" I shouted to Ayla.

She backed toward the hallway pushing Rufus behind her. "Run, child!" she screamed, but the boy stood frozen.

With one more explosive kick, the door gave way and a tall, stocky thug burst through, cold blue cheeks and black eyes. He aimed at me and called, "Guns on the floor!" When I didn't move, a bullet blasted past my shoulder, smashing into the shelves behind me. "Put yer guns down!"

I leaned over slowly, all the while watching him as I laid my rifle and pistol on the planks and pushed them in his direction.

Didier had edged into the corner of the room near Ayla, and the man jutted his chin at him. "Don't be movin', you old coot!" He swung the revolver hard. "Stay where you stand!" The man flexed his arms and hunched forward. He took two strides and reached Ayla.

"Give me the boy," he said, grabbing for the child.

Ayla's face was bloodless. "You leave this boy be!" she growled from the back of her throat. She pushed against the man's chest, throwing the weight of her body onto him.

He stumbled back, releasing Rufus. Quickly, he lifted his revolver and swung it at Ayla, knocking her to the ground.

I lunged for my guns, but the man rose to his knees and circled the heavy muzzle around the room, stopping at the sight of me.

Didier stretched tall and brazen. He pulled the derringer from his waistband, and squeezed his murder eye to a tiny slit.

"*Sale pignouf!*" He spat the insult, and the bullet exploded from the barrel, sinking into the man. Didier stood over the body without speaking, checking its limbs and chest for movement, and then kicked it hard.

"Take the boy and leave," I said to Ayla. "There'll be others coming."

Before she could move, a shadow, some worthless ribbon of God, fluttered at the yard window. Rufus saw it and screamed, and Ayla drew him close.

The yard door hung by a single hinge, swinging across the

opening from dark to light, and back into dark again. Over the threshold crossed the solitary Tom Broc, a pistol clenched in his right fist and a furnace of sweat dripping down the black Coushatta tattoo on his cheek.

He stared at the body sprawled across the floorboards. "That detective was a friend of mine. Known him since Tampico." Looking at each of us, staring at our faces and our hands, he paused when he saw the worn walnut stock of Didier's derringer. "It was you shot him?" Frowning, he shook his head, aimed his pistol, and let the bullet blast into the Frenchman's chest. Didier crumpled slowly to his knees, eyes wide open. Broc pulled the trigger again, this bullet opening the old man's neck just below the ear. He lifted the derringer from where it had fallen to the floor, and cocked it admiringly, while Ayla screamed and ran to the body.

I lurched for my weapons, but Broc spun round to me. "Oh no," he said, knocking me down. He stepped forward, planting his right foot on my wrist, splaying my hand and fingers open. Shifting his weight to hold my hand to the floor, he pointed the silvery snub down and squeezed the trigger.

I knew I had been harmed with that deafening shot, so close and carefully aimed, but I felt nothing; I saw Broc's lips move, but I heard nothing. Finally, he took a step back and handed me his bandana.

Dazed and obedient, I reached for it, but when I saw my outstretched fingers, I understood. Blood covered them, soaking my sleeve and puddling across the floor. My arm shook uncontrollably, and I wrapped his kerchief gently around my palm, pulling it across to the stump that remained of my finger.

"You'll need to stay that flow," he said, "or your pa'll never forgive me."

Broc touched my shoulder, pulling at me to rise, but the pain shot from my hand now up my arm, and the blood, having saturated his cloth, dribbled again onto the oak floor and welled in the plank seams.

"Mister Ives is dying!" Rufus shouted.

"Nah, he's not, you stupid boy. Be more'n my life's worth to kill that one. I just incapacitated him." He pulled at me again and brought me to my feet, shoving me toward the barroom. "Come along, all of you. I'll be needing a gulp of something kindly after all that kerfuffle."

I shut my eyes to the scalding pain and allowed myself to be heaved through the doorway where he kicked me into a chair. He pulled a narrow hemp rope from his belt loops and wrapped it round my wrists, tying me down, while my left hand throbbed with the pain of a thousand sharpened nails. I began to hear small insects breathing around my head. I saw nothing, but heard them still. I yanked my hands to slap them away, screaming at the luminous agony as the muscles in my wrists and fingers jerked back against the ropes.

Broc tied my ankles together, and once he had secured me to the chair, he leaned into me and tore open my shirt so that he could see the pale flesh of my chest.

"There, boy. Move again and father or not, I'll shoot you right there." He prodded my breastbone with his fingers. "Right where I see that scummy heart." He walked to the fireplace and kicked through the cold ashes. "Chilly in here, bitch," he said to Ayla. "Dontcha warm up your joint?"

The woman looked toward his voice, but called out, "Rufus, where are you?"

The boy, crouched in the far corner by the boarded-up doors, said timidly, "Here, ma'am."

Ayla walked behind the bar, her hand trailing the counter. She put her fingertips to her cheeks to wipe away tears, but when she stood before the painting of the wolf cub, she lifted her head like a damp rose to sunlight.

"You mentioned a drink, constable?"

"Yah. I'll have your finest whiskey. The pure kind, and not the shite you've been serving me all these months."

She reached down into the shelves below the counter.

"Stop!" he shouted. "Don't move. You think I don't know where your man kept his bar guns?" Broc rounded the counter, and shoved her aside. He leaned over, examining the shelves, searching every shadow of the cupboards until he was satisfied.

She grabbed a cloth and wiped it across the counter, then again; softly then rougher in some earthly delight until Broc slammed his pistol down across her arm.

"Whiskey, then. Your best one."

She lifted a small bottle from the lowest shelf, clear glass with a slight purplish tinge. "This one is from Paris. Kentucky, that is. Didier kept it for himself." She put her fingers on the bottle neck and felt for the protruding cork. She pulled hard at it until we heard the seal pop, and then turned slowly, facing the painting. Putting both hands on the counter, she slid them toward a small mirror propped against the wall. Finding a pygg clay tumbler, she took a deep breath and turned back to him. She angled the bourbon bottle over it, listening to the pour until she had filled his mug.

"There," she whispered.

"Wait," Broc said. "I want a proper glass, not that cup of a whore. Got any crystal?" He snickered before she could answer. "No, don't suppose you do, girl."

She pushed the drink toward him until it butted against his hand, and carefully, her fingertips grazed his own, and for a second, rested against them.

He gazed at her awkwardly, then opened his fingers, and pressed hers.

"I'm not a fool," he said. "I known plenty of bawds like you. I ain't gonna drink your pour unless you test it for me first. Go on, you'll be first, just to make sure. Take yerself a big gulp a' this drink."

I saw Rufus move even before I heard his sound; the boy crept from the corner toward the kitchen, and once out of the light he began to run, his shoes pounding and his small face mad with risk.

"Run, boy!" she called out, but Broc had already shifted. Strong and ready, he caught the child's sleeve, then his pantleg, and finally dragged him across the floor back to the barroom.

"Did you think I'd let you escape? You're the reason for all this, don't ya know?"

Rufus held his breath. Broc lifted the child high above his head and shoved his body down onto the floor.

Turning back to Ayla, he said, "Go on, then. Pour yerself plenty a' that whiskey."

"Rufus?" she called out. "Where're you?" With her parted lips showing thickened, red gums, Ayla waited for his answer, but the boy didn't move or speak.

"Something wrong?" Broc asked. "You afraid of it? Drink with me, girl. You people are worthless, ya know?" He glanced at me. "I been snakin' your shite all my life. And yer fuckin' father's nothin' but a thief for Gould. Didja know that, boy? If I hadn't put the fire to that Schmidt's place, he woulda' been sent to the almshouse. All a' yer stinkin' family. And you," he pointed back at Ayla, "think yer too good for me? Yer no lily, girl. Just another tramp." He grabbed her hand and squeezed it hard. "Pour it!"

She hesitated, then turned back to the wolf cub and felt for another tumbler. As she poured, she whispered, "This was Didier's favorite." In a dark and dazzling voice, she added, "His own reserve." She lifted it to her lips, gulped, and smacked it down on the counter.

Broc raised his eyebrows, putting one hand to the old black marks on his cheek. He rubbed the tattoo hard, and stared at

Ayla. Smirking, he grabbed his mug and downed the bourbon. "Oh, that is good. Sweet, even. Your husband always was a miserly codger." Wiping his mouth, he grabbed the boy by his shoulder. "I'll be back." He pushed the boy in front of him, through the kitchen doorway, stumbling slightly as he crossed the jamb.

"Stop!" I shouted, but waves of pain spun out across my hands and arms, and helpless, I fell back into the chair.

Ayla lifted her hand to her eyes. Suddenly, her fingers clenched. "Don't worry," she whispered, folding her hands tightly together and pressing them to the bar countertop. Her shoulders trembled, she faltered forward, and recklessly, she lifted her head and smiled.

CHAPTER 27

"**A**knife, Ayla! A knife to cut the ropes."

Her head lay on the counter, and her hands had turned the color of blue cream. I called her name again, but she didn't speak. She lifted her head and turned it, and as she did her tongue coiled and slid in and out of her mouth.

My own heart tightened until I could scarcely breathe. Pulling at the hemp, I tried to stand from the chair. "A knife," I whispered. But her eyes had shut, and her arms and legs juddered. I lurched again and again against the knots as one of them slackened. Leaning over, I bit at it, spitting at its center until my own saliva greased the braid looser and looser until it slipped entirely and my hands were free. I reached to the counter to take Ayla's fists, but they were limp as pulp.

I squeezed her hand, shaking it hard. Dark seams of sweat marked her sleeves and bodice, while her flesh underneath shivered like a swarm of eels. She raised her right arm and brought it down, slamming across the counter and crashing a clay crock to the floor. Her eyes opened, and slowly her cheeks drained of color. Her lips, puffed and dough-white in the candlelight, parted. Her pulsing body grew still as I watched. I'd always pitied Ayla her poor, useless eyes while she lived, but they glowed now, brave and impregnable as the deep cerulean sea.

A small blue body of shadow moved toward me, carrying what appeared to be smoldering light. I raised my right hand to strike it, but perceived the soft angles of a face, the boy again, tucking a rough hilt in my palm.

"Mister Ives?" Rufus whispered. "Here's a knife for ya." Shouldering manhood, he waited quietly while I cut the ties at my wrist and ankles.

He stood so near, I could hear his breath and feel his body, warm as steam. He didn't move, but only stared at Ayla. The clock and the world in him long ago broken, this small boy might have been jammed dead in an attic somewhere but for her.

"She dead?" he asked.

"She is," I said. "We need to be quick. We can see to her body after we find Olenbush and Stella. Broc chasing you?"

"Nah, he ain't even walkin'," the boy said. "Fell over on Soledad like all his bones're broke. Tried to get back up coupla' times, but jes' started shakin'. Laid there not sayin' nothing."

"Come here, child," I said. I held him as the shadows tumbled over us, and he nuzzled his face into my chest like a wild, newborn beast. "You're free of him, then."

"How?"

"Ayla took care of him. That woman was fiercer than all the rest of us put together." The rain had begun then, hard and steady over the front boards. I released the boy, and he leaned back to listen. "Did you see Pinks on your way here? Or police?"

"No."

"What door did you come through?"

"The broke one in the kitchen."

I took his hand and this time he came easily. "Just stay with me."

"When're Miss Moore and Mister Olenbush comin'?" he asked, but I didn't answer.

In the kitchen, we sat together in shadows. I chambered a round in the rifle and pointed it toward the open doorway.

"Your hand needs *curandero,*" Rufus whispered. "My mama is dead or she could help. Did you know she died?" He crouched beside me, and in the ochre candlelight, his shoulders appeared twisted. He held his own hand up for me to see. "We got the same hands now, don't we?"

"Yes, we do," I said. "I guess we do."

"But I can still shoot a Colt just like you. My brother taught me. Before he died." He tapped his lips together as though in thirst, but asked for nothing; he was such a beautiful child, shy even. "How do we know how long we got to live?" he asked.

I put my hand on his back, gathering the cotton in my fingers. I stroked up and down his spine, thinking this might be comfort but all I felt was a brittle root where the bone should have been. I could snap it with my one hand; anyone could.

"No one knows," I said. "That's the mystery."

"Miss Ayla told me lots of secrets. She's gone now, so I'll tell you if you want to know."

I held the rifle level again, pointing it at the black center of night outside the door. "What secrets?"

"I know where Mister Didier kept his bank."

"What bank?"

He lifted his chin high, the grain of his throat marked with old wounds. "I know," he replied loudly. "In between the ice." He smiled suddenly, boldly like a zealot.

"Ice?"

"They got ice rooms in the cellar."

"You've seen them?"

He nodded. "Ever'time when they closed at night, they hid cash money and silver. In the blocks. They wanted to take me to California. Miss Ayla said I could be her eyes."

"Did you want to go with her?"

"No, I'm goin' with Peter and Miss. And you, if you wanna come too. We're all goin' to California soon as they get back." He paused and put his harmed hand on mine. "This hurtin' you now?"

"Can't feel it anymore, son."

"Why d'ya think all of 'em wanna go to California?" he asked. "Nothin' wrong with Texas, is there?" That thought from that boy seized me, for so much about Texas had discarded him, tangled and alone, across its geography.

"Plenty of folks get rich in California," I said. "I had an uncle who went west. Years ago. He got lost, I hear. Killed a thief and ended up in jail in San Diego, but not until he pulled a fortune out of a mine. Lucky fellow, at least for a while."

"Like your pa?"

My heart thumped. A Leviathan might be clever but never lucky. "My father? No, my father never depended on luck. Who told you about my father?"

"Miss Ayla. Said he came to town to do some comeuppance."

"Go light some more lamps, Rufus. We'll be needing them soon as the others get here."

The child took a wick and carried it to the closest lantern, holding it and waiting while it flamed. He stared at the fire patiently.

"When did you go down to the ice blocks?" I asked.

"Didi took me. My mama was doctoring Ayla and he needed me to carry his money bags." The extra lampwicks had caught, and Rufus handed a lantern to me.

"He let you tote his night's profits?"

Sharply, he said, "He trusted me. And he had big crates to take down."

"Money crates?"

"All kinds."

"How does one get down there?"

"Ya gotta find the right stairs first. That's the hard part. There's little ones behind the store room. And it's real cold, too. All a' them rooms down there're cold."

"I expect that's the point, Rufus. If he keeps ice in them."

"He's got lotsa little rooms. They're all cold, but not all a' them have ice." He stared at me close for my reaction. "One has nails and knives. Some shooters, even. An' the walls and floors are all mud, all freezed up mud. My mama said I was born in a place like that."

"You weren't born in San Antonio? Where then?"

"Don't know for sure. Mama got me from the Lipans and they said I was two years old. She paid fifty dollars for me. But she didn't know where they got me. Maybe the Otter people."

"Purchasing humans isn't legal anymore," I said. "Even children."

"My mama said that's why I cost so much. Said it's hard to find babies these days."

"Well, you'll never be sold again, boy. Not while you're with us."

Rufus jerked his head away from me, away from the sooty kitchen table and the dark yard. He lurched round, staring at the bar, and rubbed his fingers roughly on his trousers. "Heard something," he said. "What was that?"

"Just the night wind. Or maybe Peter and Stella coming."

"I say it was an owl. Miss Ayla told me one of 'em got trapped in the cellar once. Died down there. Said she found its skin."

"Bird skin?" I asked, smiling faintly, until a faraway cry

shivered across us. "I think I'll block up this door. Then you can show me those ice rooms."

Without a hammer to secure the broken door, we lodged the old white table end up against the jamb to cover the opening. The boy brought the chairs to stack against it, and I dragged the iron cooking cauldrons to finish our pathetic blockade. "How'll Mister Olenbush get in when they come?" he asked.

"This won't really keep anyone out," I said. "But maybe we can slow down the ones who mean us harm."

Gravely, as though Rufus'd been touched by an apparition, he raised his harmed hand for me to follow him.

CHAPTER 28

At the far end of the storage hall, a sod floor led to a hatch, and beneath it, we teetered on three unfinished wood steps not more than a foot wide. Below those was a slippery mud staircase, colder the deeper we descended. At the bottom, we stood in a dark, low room, the sawdust-covered dirt floor coated with black, melting ice. The air hung heavy with the tantalizing sweet odor of raw wood, and an ice-awl lay in a pile of shavings at my feet. Rufus grabbed it, thrusting it as he marched like a child at play with a toy sword.

No frozen blocks had been stored here, but crates of nails were shoved against the walls. I moved my lantern across the darkness, looking for guns or ammunition boxes. Stepping closer, I stooped to flick through the nails and found an ancient rifle hidden at the bottom.

"Never was no money here," Rufus said. He stood before a small door and pulled at the knob. "This way." He stepped forward and disappeared through the purple shadows, and the blue, and finally into the silence and the black.

A moment passed, and at last his voice bounded against the walls of a far storeroom. "I can't see. My lamp's out."

"Stay where you are and I'll come to you." I found an open doorway to a small passage where leaves of ice hung down the walls like silver. "Did you find the money?" I called.

"No. Just more crates."

"Keep talking," I said. "I'm almost there. Do you see my light?"

Before he could answer, I saw his outline: a child sitting on a simple box, staring at the abyss beyond. He didn't move when I approached.

"I'm here, Rufus." I lifted his shivering body and saw that the crate where he had stopped was stuffed with dusty books and packages of yellowed pages, tied with string and iced together like the wings of a dying cicada.

I lit the boy's lamp from my own, and brought his body close, both of us squirming together for warmth.

"I saw the moon on the ceiling," he whispered, and closed his eyes.

"There's no moon down here, Rufe."

He'd begun to cry against the bitter air. "My arms're on fire!"

"When it's so cold, your skin becomes too hot," I said. "Like it's burning. It's normal. Caused by your blood slowing down."

I rubbed his limbs, pressing harder and rubbing faster until he cried out, "Stop! You're hurting me!"

"I'm sorry, boy. Maybe we should go back upstairs." I pulled a packet of papers from the crate beside us and untied the string, wrapping them around his arms and hands for insulation. "And get out of this cold."

"We gotta get the money first. We be close, Mister Ives!" He tore the pages from around his limbs, and dashed toward the next doorway. I held my lamp high, the light exposing a dark swath of blood smeared down his shirt.

"Rufus, come back! You're bleeding!" But he scampered into the next room, leaving behind only a small moon of shivering light. And then I saw across the pages in my hand that a thick stream of blood dripped from my bandage.

"Come with me!" he called. "I found the ice blocks!"

I stood from the crate to follow, but sat back immediately. Unable to hold my head up, pain shooting through my temples, I slumped onto the icy straw-covered floor. I thought I heard movement above my head, steps soft as moccasins. The padding stopped, the timbre of a man's voice echoed, and my eyelids drooped closed.

~

When I awoke, Rufus stood over me holding a chunk of ice. Peter knelt beside him, staring at me and waiting while Stella handed him a clay cup. Together, they lifted my head to drink.

"It's just sugar water," she said.

I let some slide down my throat. "I'm fine. Just lost a little more blood than I could spare, I guess." I smiled wanly and looked down at my hand. The old bandage was gone, replaced with clean, unbleached muslin that had been wrapped round my palm and finger stump.

"Lean John against the crate," Stella said. "He needs to be straight-sitting to breathe properly."

Peter obeyed her while I took the cup in my good hand. "You been out a while," he said. "Doc Herff's on his way." He reached for the ice block. "What ya got there, Rufe?"

"Some a' Didier's money! A roomful back there." He pushed the block toward Peter. "Look! I'm not lyin'."

Peter put it on the floor where the cold water seeped to mud at our feet. The block was made of two smaller slabs frozen together. Between these lay a bag, lodged in the ice.

"Here y'ar," Rufus said, handing him the awl. "There's treasure in that sack."

Peter took the tool and lifted it high, then struck down hard into the core. The chunk split open, revealing jagged frozen cracks surrounding a coarse pouch. He tugged at the stiff cloth while chipping at it from side to side until it came free. He loosened its ties and pushed his hand inside. Pulling his fist from the bag, Peter opened his fingers to reveal large, thick coins.

"See!" cried Rufus. "Silver 'n' gold!"

"Indeed," I said, and lifted some of the money into my fists.

"And there's more in that room. Loads and loads more. We be rich now!"

"This isn't our money, child," Stella said.

"Well, whose then?" I asked. I put my hand tentatively against the wall for balance and stood up. "How long till the doc arrives?"

Peter shrugged, bending to the crate where I had been leaning. Some of the papers had fallen on the muddy straw, and he picked them up, wiping them on his trousers.

"What's that?" I asked.

"Some old saloon records," he said.

"Only good for burning now. Although the crates could be useful."

Peter dropped to his knees. "No, we'll take these with us."

"Let me see," I said, and he handed a page to me, columns of numbers itemizing amounts taken and amounts paid.

"Yah, we'll take these," he said and grabbed the paper from me. Above us, the thuds of a fist beat on wood, and a distant voice called out several times. Peter folded the ledger page and slipped it quickly into his pocket. "Doc Herff is here."

"How do you know?" I asked. "Could be the Pinks."

"Now that Broc is dead, I doubt they'll be arrivin' so soon. Besides, I told our doc to come through the back yard." He put his hand to Stella's soiled collar, allowing his fingertips to drift up her neck. "I'll go up and make sure. Y'all stay in this room until I call you. Then bring Johnny upstairs."

When Doctor Herff unwrapped the bandages, my hand was as wrinkled as a leaf. He laid the soiled muslin on a table in the taproom and sat me at a chair alongside. He pulled a roll of cotton fiber from his bag, grumbling in German as he did, and soaked the batting in carbolic acid. Working quickly, he swept my entire hand with the cotton, covering the stump for a few seconds.

"Tell me if it starts to hurt. Prolonged pain might be lethal." I considered that to be poor humor from an educated man, until I noticed he didn't smile. I took a deep breath and looked away but he was adroit and experienced, and the disinfecting didn't cause me to jolt. The carving and sanding of my splintered bone did, though, and likewise the silk stitching of my skin, which were most certainly the causes of my second loss of consciousness that eve. By the time I opened my eyes, he was gone and my hand had been wrapped and tied off with great precision.

"Whiskey?" Peter asked. We sat alone in the kitchen, a new single-shot Springfield rifle in his hands.

I nodded. "Now that your doctor has fiddled with my fingers, the pain is worse than ever. Pounding hard. All over my body."

"That's the glory of docs. 'Specially the Prussian ones." He filled a tumbler and handed it to me. "We need to leave tonight. Think you can make the ride?"

"I can. Just not sure I want to." I gulped the cup empty.

"We can't wait, Johnny. Better to get out in the dark while they're seein' to Broc's body."

"I wouldn't ask you to stay. But I don't think I'll be going along. You and Stella and her sister, that's your life now. I still got some things to sort here."

"We'll be takin' the wagon out back, and our horses. The crates, and weapons we find, and the money. And the bodies, Didier and Ayla. Give 'em a good burial once we fetch the girl. I could make use of your help, even one-handed as you are."

"Do you understand how she died?" I asked.

"Rufus said she suffered some kinda convulsion. Said it was similar to how Broc passed over on Soledad."

"That's true. A little more complicated, though. A secret gift, it was."

Peter's eyes narrowed. "What was?" he asked, his voice low and hard like gravel.

"Broc demanded whiskey and she poured it for him. But it seems that particular bottle had an extra ingredient. Thought he was clever, and made her drink before he did. He never believed the woman had mettle. Just thought she was like him and never imagined she could see light in her death." I gaped at him as the sound of my words faded.

"She saved you and the boy?"

"Correct." The rain had softened to mizzle. I stared around that tainted room, at the four lamps that burned in each corner, at the little gleaming crosses that lay on the table. And when I turned back to Peter, he was watching me from the shadows. "I'll come with you to bury her. Of course she deserves that."

CHAPTER 29

As single cart track led through the woods to the fork of the rivers, its slushy mud foul as soupy cud and guts. Our wheels sank easily into this earth, and the horses were unable to pull us out.

"Might as well go on foot now," Peter said, tethering the animals to the surrounding trees. "We're close enough."

"I can go on my own to fetch Lucy. One of us needs to stay here to protect the others."

I slipped from my ride to follow the softened ruts forward out of the tree cover.

"Can you call to the marsh people to come and help us?" Stella asked.

"Of course," I said, but their camp was oddly quiet, and already I was unsure what I might find. The morning twilight after the rain had spread the sky with indigo, and as I emerged from the deep night I saw that the bog was glassy as a pond—and empty.

Standing under the moon and the mist, I observed neither human nor animal. "Gone," I called back. "No wagons. No souls."

Peter scrambled through the mud to where I stood, staring onto the marsh. "Not even the girl?" he asked. Without waiting for my answer, he walked into the swampy meadow, sinking to his ankles in the grasses and slush. He paused near a fallen log and bent over, pulling something free, twisting and yanking at the soggy bark. "A shag of torn cloth," he called, then moved again to the bankside, stooping to collect the other remnants of life the marsh people had left behind.

Stella and the child rushed from the woods through the reeking rainwater, coming to a stop beside me. "Where are they?" she asked. "Was it a slaughter? Lord, where's my sister?"

"No sign of killing, but Peter's searching. It seems they've all disappeared."

Furious and glittering in the rain and the dawn, she caught up to Peter at the top of the bank near the sodden firepit. He turned to her, his arms wide, dropping everything in his hands. They embraced for a long time, her head against Peter's breast.

"Where's the marsh folks?" Rufus asked finally, but Stella had begun to weep and I didn't answer.

Rufus clenched his eyebrows tight together, and bit down on his lower lip. "I don't understand. What's wrong with Miss? They still marryin'?"

I pulled a blue rag from my pocket and cupped the child's chin in my palm. "Of course, son." Wiping mud off his cheeks, I said again, this time firmly. "Of course. She's sad that her sister is gone, but they'll be marrying and taking you to California, certainly." I shoved the curls from his forehead to wipe it, but before I could, he spoke again.

"How d'you know? I always been trouble. Easy for people to change once they know."

"Nonsense," I said. "You're a fine, smart boy and you'll have a good life."

A pinky spoonbill came down from the freezing sky and

landed on the silent marsh, striking the water with force. Off its migratory path, it trawled for familiar food that did not exist here, scooping again and again until it lifted its broad wings, threw its shoulders back, and took flight up through the gray.

I put my hands on the child and turned him away from the sight of Peter and Stella. Leading him toward our horses and the settlement of riches that lay in the wagon, I said, "Let's count those coins and repack them while we wait."

He climbed upon the bench and we sat side by side tallying up. Every so often he scrambled back into the box to fetch another bag of coins from between the bodies. Each time he did, I saw him put his fingers on Ayla's forehead, barely touching her skin, but moving his lips as he told her some secret. And when he put the bags in my hands, he fixed a little frown on his face, perhaps for her death or for the people he had already lost; perhaps even for himself, a boy of so much trouble.

Stella and Peter didn't return until the morning sun crested the horizon, and when they came to us they did not mention Lucy.

"Let's get this wagon out," Peter said sharply, and began to build mounds of soil and branches under the wheel felloes. His lips were clamped together and he walked past me to fetch more brush.

He returned with an armful of twigs and leaves, and without a word, stuffed them into the crevices beneath the rims.

"That box of ledgers in the cart, we could use some of those for traction," I said. "They'd work better than soggy leaves."

He lifted his face, his green eyes catching the cold sunlight, and pushed his jaw forward. "No. I'm savin' those for other uses."

I knelt beside him and asked softly, "What do you imagine happened to the camp? Any clues that might guide us to Lucy?"

He looked at me without expression. "Girl was no gift to anyone. I'm thinkin' we're at last free of her."

"She was a gift to her family, to Stella, don't you think?"

He slipped a knife from his boot and began scraping it back and forth across a field stone to sharpen the blade. "No," he said simply, and laid the blade against a fistful of branches. So easily, he pulled the steel down the stems, skinning the ends easily. "Said she wanted to stay with those folks, wanted to travel with them. So she did. Not even a final goodbye to her sister, after everything Stella's done. All that worry for a hag who didn't even care."

I put my hands into the shallow pools beside us, pulling up more decaying leaves and reeds. The stench of rot clung to my skin as I shook the drops from them and handed them over.

"Maybe she didn't run again. Maybe the marsh people even forced her. Are you not intending to seek her out?"

"That's right, Johnny. Stella and I gotta start our life now. Can't keep chasin' that girl, can we? Stella agrees with me."

"She does?" I asked, but he didn't answer.

He stood tall, like a night traveler on the edge of light, considering a response. Calmly, he asked, "You helpin'?" He leaned against one of the wheels and gestured at the other. "Stella, get up on the bench and drive this rig, please." She followed his instructions and the two of us put our shoulders to the rims. "On my count then. One! Two! Three!"

At his last shout, Stella snapped the reins across the backs of the horses while Peter and I heaved into the weight of the wagon. All three of us bellowed, bawling louder at the animals as they staggered up the mounds of earth and grass and sodden brush, until at last I felt the car lurch hard as the horses found firm ground. Peter and I leaned back and watched while Stella deftly drove forward.

"Going about!" she shouted, then, "Yah!" as she turned the

wagon back into the woods. Once on the track again, she pulled up on the reins, and the horses slowly came to a halt.

"We should be makin' our way to the cemetery," he said.

"The cemetery? You think that's wise to bury them in such a public place?" I asked.

"Gotta put 'em in the ground," he said, wiping the sweat from his neck.

"Why not inter them here?"

Stella remained on the bench holding the reins in her lap. "This is hardly hallowed ground, John."

"Maybe not, but in San Antonio not much is blessed by God these days. Here's just as pure, and probably safer for us while we do the burying."

Idly, she put a hand to a new chain at her throat, pressing it between thumb and forefinger. "And you would bless this swamp somehow?"

"Who am I to bless anything, Stella? Any of us for that matter."

"What will it be, then?" She looked straight at Peter. "The cemetery or here?"

"I think we bury them in these woods, girl," he said. "Where no one will see us, and folks won't find 'em for a long time. Johnny's right. We can't risk workin' on the open hill so near town."

We had neither wood nor caskets, but we had brought sheets from the Silver King rooms to wrap the bodies. A couple of hours passed as Peter and I dug with makeshift tools, deep enough to hide the scent from even the most ravenous wolf. At last with the diggings complete, we stood on two sides of the single hole, our hatless heads uncovered against the wind, while Peter used his bare hands to roll the bodies down.

Stella began the consecration by singing the Portuguese Hymn, only the first two verses because she had forgotten most of the words beyond the citizens of heaven. She took to humming, strong and sweet, then stopped, leaving deep stillness between us.

"Who will speak for them?" she asked, her shoulders shaking. "I cannot."

"Nope," said Peter. "I'm not the one to do it. Besides, Johnny's had the best schooling."

The two turned to me, and reluctantly I scooped fistfuls of mud in my hands, tossing the glop onto the bodies of Ayla and Didier as they lay together.

"They saved us several times," I said, and then invoked a heaven in which I held no faith for their protection.

Rufus stepped forward to where I stood and bent to the mound of soil. I thought he would toss it and walk away, but once he stood, he turned to us, looking at each of our faces, one by one. "I'll talk," he said fiercely, and then threw the mud into the hole. "These was my friends. They fed me sometimes, and Miss Ayla, well she tol' me she got nothin' left." He picked a stone from the ground, examined it, and slipped it into his pocket. "Ain't fair. She warn't nobody's jobber. They tried to hush 'er but she din't let 'em." He bent again to push more soil into the hole, and Peter rounded the grave to help him. "She had more'n all of us in 'er blood."

When they had finished, Peter held a hand to the boy. "Come here, Rufe. We been buryin' too many folks lately. I say enough. What you say?"

Rufus nodded. "Enough, sir." Both impenitent, they marched to the wagon together and Peter lifted him onto the bench.

CHAPTER 30

Peter took the reins from Stella and sat alongside her, while Rufus squatted on the planks among the crates and valises.

"If I'm rememberin' correctly," I said, "a train west leaves tomorrow morning. Though we'd need to find rooms to stay tonight. Safe lodging, if such a thing exists for us in San Antonio." I rode along the rutted track beside them, enough ahead so that they couldn't see my expression nor determine my thoughts. "It heads to Spofford Junction and from there you can get to El Paso and on to Los Angeles." My words and my voice, so boyishly eager, made me cringe.

"That's the Texas Pacific line that Gould and your father own," Peter replied. "That your idea of safe? San Antonio station is probably overrun with Pinkertons seekin' us out already."

"Actually, we could ride to Spofford on horseback and get the train from there," Stella suggested.

"Either way, it's a dog's game, ain't it?" At the gruff sound of his voice, she put her hand on Peter's forearm, and he fell silent, staring at her flesh.

"Will you be joining us on to California, John?" she asked.

"No, I don't think so."

"Where will you go?"

"Who knows?" I replied. "With the funds we've acquired, I suppose I'll take my share and be finding my way back to my home in Boston." Peter glared at me and I knew I'd been trapped in a pathetic lie. What home did I have anymore? A soft fellow like me could yearn for a pool of shade but that yearning could never be called home.

"Be a few hours to town," he said. "We'll divvy up on the way. Won't take long to get a price for the rig and animals, unless you'll be needing 'em, Johnny."

"Just my ride here," I said, fondling the horse's mane while it raised its head and pinned its ears back flat to its neck.

"That road to Spofford, that's a rough road," Peter said. "Might not be suitable for you, darling."

She held herself straight and tall, leaning away from him. "What wouldn't be suitable for me is seeing Pinkerton officers gather round and shoot you dead."

We hit a long, straight stretch of open road where the mud had crusted already. Peter stamped on the footrest and howled at the horses to kick them even faster.

"Stop, please," Stella said calmly. "You're frightening us. Such a miscreant."

He opened his mouth wide and laughed into the wind. Squaring his shoulders, he busted the reins hard, and shouted, "Hold my arm, sweetheart!"

"You'll never change!" she shouted, but she laughed as well and reached a hand back to Rufus.

"No, I don't suppose I will!"

I pulled up on my horse and watched them gallop down the trace, none of them caring a whit for catastrophe in those last, few wild moments. They bore down the trail past me and Peter lifted one hand into the air, waving it brashly, and as he did, I could see that his nails were the color of butter.

Rufus crawled toward the bench and flung his thin chest across Peter's back, slinging his arms around his neck. Slicks of mud spattered into the air, while unbound ledger pages from the wagon rose on the gusts and dropped to the weeds. At the edge of a lea clearing, Peter circled the horses out and called them to slow.

I squeezed my own horse forward to a four-beat. Listening to the winter wind-birds in the tops of the oaks surrounding us, while a red-tailed hawk circled the sky above them, I picked my way on and off the trail, avoiding the yellowed pages of the old balance sheets that had blown from the wagon box. So many scattered the ground that I slipped down and grabbed several that I found sticking together at my feet.

"Look here!" I shouted. "You've lost some of your precious papers. Let's just hope you didn't lose us any of our cash as well!"

Peter turned back to me and halted the horses. Pulling the brake, he leapt from the wagon and raced back to where I stood, snatching the sheets from the mud as he went. By the time he faced me, he held an armful. I looked from the pages to his face; his cheeks were red and sweating, his eyes lifeless as green glass.

He reached for what I had gathered, but I didn't move and didn't breathe. What I held between my fingers was an accounting ledger, at the top of which, swirled in roundhand script were these words:

International Railway Improvement Company.
1 April 1881 through 30 June 1881.
Boston, Massachusetts.

I scanned to the bottom. To most, it was a page of chicken

scratches, but to me, terrifying black ink, fading and smeared from years of storage. The columns of numbers on a single sheet totaled over twenty-five thousand dollars.

Peter reached toward me again, taking the corner of my page in his muddy fingertips, and this time I let it slip away. "I don't understand," I said. "This belonged to one of my father's companies."

His eyes were sharp and confident, and he stared into mine without responding.

I bowed my head, my hands falling to my sides. The space between us was vacant and full at the same time. I tried to lose the language in my head, the questions, even the little flames that leapt from me. I stood quite still and looked up at him again.

"Did Didier work for my father?" The wind and the hawk roused, so loud together that I was compelled to bellow above them, "Do you?"

"Neither of us did." He said it softly, but I heard his nettled voice all the same.

"What then? I need to understand why he kept my father's ledgers in his ice rooms."

"Didier found them after the fire. Brought 'em home. *Chantage,* he called it."

"*Chantage?*"

"Protection against Broc. The old Frenchie was blackmailing 'im for the folks Broc killed and why." He folded the page and slipped it into the pocket of his duster. "Anyone who knew about these records needed protection. Lotta people died because of your pa's damned balance sheets."

"But Tom Broc is dead. And what do these financial records have to do with anyone he killed? These are just the balance sheets of a company that ran out of funds. My father made a decision to close it down. Nothing murderous in that."

"I heard the investors lost over half a million dollars. Wonder how that happened with smart men like your pa and Gould running things. And why d'you think boxes of the accounts from an eastern company ended up in San Antonio? And why d'you think you did?"

"I've nothing to do with this company. They were building the rail down to Mexico, had some delays, lost some money, and stopped the work."

"Well, Didier had a different opinion. Said they never really got started on the rail line they'd promised. Money disappeared and weren't any sheets to show where it got spent. Except maybe in these boxes."

"That's absurd! The investors lost money. Happens all the time between these men. My father's lost plenty over the years." Yellow bell flowers grew beside the trail, their last, large flutes exposed to the wind and the frost. I pressed my lips together and snatched a blossom from its sepal shield, whirling it between my fingers until the petals fell to the ground. "Just some unsuccessful business decisions."

We heard the smack of leather shoes on the mud behind us, and Peter spun round. "Rufus, child, what're you doin'?"

"Miss tol' me to give ya' a hand." The boy began collecting the pages into a wad.

"Thanks, son," Peter said, and bent to gather the ones at his feet. "And you," he said to me, "you better be prayin' hard for the end of the killin', cuz there's others in the line of fire. Just cuz Broc is dead doesn't mean there's not a dozen Pinkertons waitin' to take his place in your father's business." Rufus ran before us, racing after the pages floating in the wind and grabbing those weighted down by lumps of mud.

"You mean the boy, I suppose."

"Anyone who's heard the truth'll be seein' angels, Johnny, if we're not careful. Me, Rufus, even Stella. Town is full a' Pinkertons workin' at your pa's pleasure."

"My father didn't kill Rufus's mother or his brother. My father didn't set that fire. That was Broc, and Ayla took care of him."

"Yes, she did. Bless her brave heart."

"And my father may have instructed havoc to fall on some rivals over his business years, but he would never harm a fine woman such as Stella. You can be certain of that."

Peter glided his right hand across the Colt on his thigh, letting it hover like a feather. "Like I said, you best be prayin' hard you're right."

If a man could be the darkest soul and the brightest at the same time, I would declare Peter that man. He bent to the ground and took the last page, then walked across the clearing back to the wagon where Stella waited in the light.

Now that the morning star had disappeared, the thick air lay about us, spreading a rich smell of moss and wood. Rufus climbed to the bench alongside Stella, and Peter took the reins.

My horse, impatient at their movement, stamped its front hooves in the mistflower, crushing it and causing the scent of vanilla to escape. I put my boot in the stirrup, grabbed the saddle horn, and pulled myself up. Watching the three, I saw how pathetic my caution was, how pathetic I was. Through the barren spirit of my family, I saw that small window, the one that sometimes opens before us. Frightened but unstoppable, I kicked the horse headlong toward them, pulling up hard and breathless at the wagon wheels. "I've decided I might accompany you to California after all," I said. "Just to look around, of course. Not a forever home," I said, smiling at Stella.

"C'mon, friend. We got miles to do before Spofford Junction."

I rode alongside them under the odd beauty of the old

persimmon trees, an avenue of unplucked black fruit rotting against milk-white branches. Emerging from these old Spanish orchards, we reached the Lower Emigrant Road at the edge of San Antonio, crossing the rail lines at the edge of town into the weak sunlight.

"One quick stop first?" I asked. "I'll ride ahead and meet you in an hour out the west side of town. If you'll wait?"

"Your pa?" he asked.

"No, but I'd like to know if Nora Nesbit survives. If there's anything I can do for her."

Peter touched his forefinger to the brim-edge of his hat, and looking straight at me, kissed the air as the horses moved forward.

crossed the tracks, those graceful, curving switches encrusted with dung and mud, blood sometimes, as well as the hairless, twining hemlock lace. The rails had been created with heat and hammers, bending now west into the desperate frontier or east, back toward the lawless Galveston gulf. Steam in witchy billows poured from an engine as it pulled away from the yard. Limp bluebonnet blossoms clung so close to the earth, growing between the rail ties and the fasteners, somehow rising yet to bloom until the next train rolled in to crush them.

As I drew closer, I spotted the rear of my father's Pullman in the distance. One fellow was polishing the sides to a black obsidian glow, while another, a lone Pinkerton, stood on the rear platform. The Pink held a rifle, resting it across the iron railing as he scanned the tracks. Even at that distance, I could tell that both manservant and gunman were new, both tentative in their occupations with rag or rifle.

What I could not see was the source of music, mellow bowing of minor chords, vulgar vibrato low and so unearthly that it prophesied decay. I followed the sound but went wide around the steel rails, turning a quick corner behind wooden cargo cars. The strings continued, surly and sensual, alarming even, but I saw no musician. And suddenly, as I peered at the Pullman again, the music stopped, and I realized it had come from within my father's coach.

I tethered my horse, took only my pistol, and skirted out, hidden until I had a full view of the private car. My father's carriage was now hunkered near the depot building, where I suppose he might observe any soul with malice who approached. I moved toward it through the fat, slick weeds between the ties. I identified only the two men working beside it, the Pinkerton poised at the back and the servant by the steps. Striding toward the second, unfamiliar in face and physique, I sank slowly into the deep, oily muscle of the earth between us.

"Ho, there!" I called. The manservant pulled a pistol from his beltline and fixed the barrel on me. "I seek my father," I said. "Mister Ives. Please inform him John is here."

Lifting his head to eye my lines, he let the muzzle dip slightly toward the mud at my feet.

"Stay where you are," he said, and called over his shoulder into the doorway. Hearing us, the Pinkerton trotted from the rear of the car to the front, and climbed up the steps to stand beside the manservant.

Hidden in the dark of the doorway, I heard my father. "Aside there," he said, his words alone parting the men. Diminutive between his towering employees, his voice was nonetheless forceful. "Ah, John. I was certain you'd capitulate." He removed his golden pince-nez from the bridge of his nose, tilting his forehead as he examined me from top to bottom. He squinted dramatically and asked, "What befell your hand?"

"Your man, Broc. Don't you know that?" I asked. I waved my bandaged palm in his face. "He shot me. Surely your people have told you. I suffered for days with the wound."

"My man, you say?" he asked, chuckling quietly.

Sprigs of barleyweed soaked in the day's rain near my boots. I took a step and bent forward, grabbing a clump, tearing at it for no purpose but to have it. "I know he's worked for you for years," I said. "That you brought him here from Galveston and had him appointed to the San Antonio police."

He waved his hand, scowling. "Nothing illegal in that."

"So you must also have been notified about his recent demise."

"Of course. That's of no consequence. That copper needed killing long ago." His mouth agape, he hooked his pale fingers across his lips, and for a moment it was as though his small blue eyes faced a deluge. "My son, I'm so pleased you've come to see me."

"I'm not here to see you. I've come to fetch Nora. She deserves to be free of you."

His eyes were wicked and red as though ripe with brandy. "Then you've come for nothing. That woman is long gone. She managed to plead a sing-song to my last servant so he paid her fare." He turned back to his new manservant and growled, "Get me my tobacco, boy."

The fellow nodded and said, "Yes sir," stepping quickly into the parlor through the carriage door.

My father's voice softened into long-practiced equanimity, a mask I knew well. "As long as you're here, John, do come in and have a drink." Lifting his hand, he summoned me forward with only three fingers, and I did climb the steps to face him. "Inside, son. We'll have a whiskey, maybe a laugh. And my violinist will play you a caprice to send you on your way to Tampico."

The wind rose hard off the river, out across the open yard, so hard that I swear I heard the canal weeping. I paused on the platform before the carriage door, taking a breath, not rising to his stubborn plan. Calmly, I asked, "Where did Nora go?"

"I've no idea. Boston? Union Square? Perhaps Chicago."

"Did she have funds? Surely she had some purse to help her."

"She left one night while I was sleeping quite soundly. I do believe the servant drugged me a bit." He shrugged. "He disappeared as well or I would have discharged him, of course."

"How do I know you didn't kill them?" I asked.

"You don't. But I've never killed anyone, not even soldiering during the Great Rebellion."

A dazzle of lies, I thought, for he had paid a man to take his place when the conscripting letter came. "You were never in the war. You're forgetting how well I know your fictions. And I remember tales of a few men and women you quieted along the way. Daniel, for one."

"Don't be ridiculous. Your brother's anatomy was death from the beginning. We all knew it," he replied, grunting to himself.

"He was your son as much as he was my brother. Of no consequence to you, of course. So you let him die."

"Be careful with your accusations." He turned his head to the parlor, and never before had I seen him this mortal. He shouted, "Play something lively, my friend!" The sound of carefree strokes danced out from a violin, and my father looked back at me, smiling darkly. The creases at the corners of his mouth dug deep, and the wrinkles at his jawline separated his limp, fleshy jowls.

Suddenly, I slipped my hand inside my jacket pocket and pulled from it a yellowed page I'd stolen from Didier's crates. I'd folded it in half, then quarters, and then eighths, folding and unfolding again and again, not certain until that moment that I would have the courage to wave it in his face.

I opened the page. "This was found in the warehouse that burned."

"What is that?" he asked slowly, his voice thin and nasal. "And where did you get it?"

"Those would be my questions for you since the name of your bankrupt company is on this sheet."

He stepped back, just inside the door where his gentleman handed him a lit cigarette. My father inhaled deep and strong before he spoke. "If you already know, you have no reason to inquire, then." He turned and went into the Pullman.

"Why would your books be in a warehouse in San Antonio?" I held the page in the air at his back. "Why would Broc set fire to them? Unless these are the ones the courts have been demanding of you?" I lurched forward, following him into the train.

Nothing had changed from my last visit, golden tray and china teapot, the jade warhorses and thick purple curtains. The parlor fireplace was stoked high, and on either side the marble glowed pink from the flames. "My bones are getting old, son," he said. "Cold all the time." He strolled to stand in front of the warmth and said coolly, "Do tell me where you found that sheet. Are there others?"

"Not until you tell me why this is in Texas and not Boston."

"Olenbush had them, didn't he? And all along I thought it was the girl who stole them from Broc. Do tell me where my documents are now. You realize the Pinkertons have a substantial reward on offer. We could take it and split it!"

"You didn't answer my question!"

"You don't ease my doubt about your ability to manage our companies when you speak to me with that disrespectful voice."

I looked away to the window and across the rail yard. A new barbed wire fence guarded the property, more efficient, some thought, than the line of cottonwoods that had sagged over the canals since the Payaya people dug them.

"I'll never be part of your industries. And I'd like to think you'll lose them all once the truth of these accounts is disclosed. Among your other crimes, you're a common thief who stole from your investors."

The door to the bedroom opened and through it, strolled a man, a fiddler from the marsh, playing a loud, sweet melody. When he saw me, he lowered the instrument from between his neck and chin, stopped walking, and nodded in recognition.

"Don't stop, friend," my father said to him.

Before he could strike the bow again, a high-pitched scream exploded from the bedroom. "What the hell?" I shouted, and rushed toward the sound. "Nora!"

My father didn't move, but merely said, "I told you Nora left days ago."

The Pinkerton lunged for me before I could cross the bedroom threshold. He grabbed my wrist and bent it back. Prying the Colt from my fingers, he flung my pistol across the railcar, where it crashed into the jade horses. The gun cracked sharply against the window, the bullet flashed, and the shattered glass showered around us. The gunman threw me to the floor and pinned me flat against the thick carpet. Groaning over me, his hands closed around my neck.

"Stop!" my father said. "Get him up and bring him along."

The man pulled me upright, his own face a patchwork of seeping blood. "Mister Ives?" he called, but my father didn't respond. Instead, he strode to the far corner of the bedroom, and the gunman, wiping the blood with his sleeve, shoved me after.

And there, surrounded by ghostly jeweled light, stood our mad, disfigured Lucy, chanting softly to the corner angels. She wore only a raw muslin shift, decorated with soiled yellow roses. Chained to the potbelly stove door, she wept and whispered, the hot iron and coal fire crackling behind her.

"No!" I shouted, throwing myself forward, wrenching hard at the Pinkerton holding me.

An iron padlock fixed her wrists to the scorching heat, and she rocked her head from side to side, shouting, "Holy secrets in the barn!" Her voice began to trill in the language of a wild bird until suddenly, she coughed hard and whispered at me, "He gave me his Bible to keep, so many ciphers but I read it all. Hail everywhere!" Her shoulders shook, and their shadows shook as well against the compartment's wall. Trembling like a river, she said, "He brought me to the snow, rubbed my face in it. He filled my throat with snow till I choked."

"Put her on the bed," my father said.

"Did you do these things to that poor girl?" I shouted. "She's ready to tell us all about you."

"Of course not."

The fiddler splayed her out, tying each wrist and ankle to a post. She screamed again, her legs convulsing while he pulled the ropes tight, her eyes desperately fixing on mine.

In one hand my father held a cigarette and in the other, a small pistol. "Here," he said, and handed his smoke to the musician, who leaned forward and pressed the burning end against the skin of Lucy's neck.

Whimpering, she clenched her eyes closed. "Please," she said, but the marsh man did not pull back.

"Stop it!" I shouted, lunging at my father, breaking away. The Pinkerton leaned toward the windows and grabbed my fingers to stop me.

"What is this woman to you?" my father called out, standing over her. He brought his hands together, creating a double fist. Lifting them over his gray scalp, he thrust his arms down, slamming into her face while her body shook as she tried to free herself. "Lie back. Keep your eyes clear and lie back, bitch."

I grabbed my father by the shoulders and pushed him away from her. "And what is she to you?"

The fiddler pulled a little Remington pistol from his pocket and pointed its thick nose at my chest.

"No!" my father shouted. "This is my son!" He stood up and brushed the folds from his jacket and trousers. "She is nobody," he said to me. "A mistake. Just someone whom I was told held something I wanted. A lie of course." He reached out to the fiddler, saying, "Give me that!" Taking the thick pistol nose from the musician, he pointed the barrel back at him. Without another word, he squeezed the trigger, and planted a bullet in the musician's neck. Turning round to the bed, he gazed at Lucy for a few moments. "She knows everything. As did that damned gypsy." With that, my father cocked the Remington again and aiming it at Lucy, put a bullet into her heart.

That man of such myth, composed in deepening clouds, leaned over the girl and smeared the blood into the hair at her temples. He stared at her wide eyes for a moment, then with his bloody fingers, parted her lips, and sank his tongue between them.

CHAPTER 32

J raced to the bed and stooped over her body. The odor
of carbolic acid and urine rose from her thighs and
around her arms. I reached for her wrist, and lay my fingers on
her pulse veins but felt no beat of blood. I looked up and found
my father staring at me, his head nodding almost in celebration.

It had been years since I believed in prayer or since I'd
attempted to protect sacred fantasies. I remembered the
shadows of my brother's cemetery where no more bodies could
be laid down. I'd never made an oath for him, never scraped my
skin for him with holly thorns. Daniel had always been at the
edge of life under the mantle of this monster, but somehow, I'd
imagined myself immune.

I stood from the girl and walked back to the parlor where my
father waited with the pistol in his hand and two thick, crystal
glasses before him.

"Now we can have a serious discussion," my father said. "Sit,
John." He placed the little Remington on the table and stroked
his lips as though to cleanse them.

"You and I will never again speak," I whispered. "About
anything."

Beside me stood the Pinkerton, rifle raised, and muzzle trained on me. Before me stood my benefactor, gulping drink to drive himself deeper. I eyed the pistol, multiplying the distance by the seconds it would take to reach it, cock it, and fire into the gunman's heart. A meager calculation that, offering a brittle margin.

I sat into an overstuffed chair and stared out the shattered window. Behind the new barbed wire, behind the trees, lay a large pool of gathered rain, and bent over it knelt a blond fellow cupping water to his mouth. He drank but did not stand again, his face seemingly focused on mine though I well knew he couldn't see me. Slowly then, I realized that I was watching Peter as he, in turn, watched the railcar.

Whiskey in hand, my father strutted back and forth, rambling from one topic to another. "You don't understand. You've never worked for anything, John, but the fine industrialist I am today is because of my hard work and business sense." His gentleman walked beside him, a fellow of youth and thin, gangly limbs, filling the glass again and again. "Take the Tampico effort, the one that you abandoned…"

"I left with malaria, if you remember."

"But was it malaria, really? Or was it just too much for you?" The tawny color of his cheeks now flushed his entire face, and his voice grew louder. "Those dimwitted jungle Huastecos believed the tar pools there were only good for gluing their canoes! All that oil. It took a man like me to show them. I was the one for the job, while you were commiserating with your brother in Boston. Such sad boys with such a cruel father! What a chuckle that was! I was the better man with the better intellect, while the two of you showed yourselves as self-possessed weaklings."

He spoke with such force that spittle had gathered at the corner of his mouth. "Daniel deserved to die," he sighed, and turned to his new, clumsy manservant. "Boy!" he called out suddenly.

The young fellow offered a clean handkerchief to my father, who tore it from his hand.

"My brother died because of you!" I said. "And you did nothing to help him. Just watched him fall."

Oblivious, he threw the kerchief to the carpet and nodded at the servant to pick it up. "Daniel deserved to die," he repeated, "just like those damned dock jimmies at Galveston."

"You're a thief as well as a murderer. You stole hundreds of thousands of dollars from your investors. Took their dreams and their money and used it all for your own ends."

"Dreams?" he laughed, turning to me. "Don't be ridiculous. The only dream a businessman has is the dream of more. There was never any naïveté about their investments," he hissed. "You would believe my partners who turned on me, over a father who protected you all your life?"

At the doorway to the bedroom compartment, he stopped suddenly and wheeled round to face the servant. The man leaned back as though to avoid a strike, and my father shouted, "For God's sake, go and clear the body from my chamber before the smell of that woman overtakes us!"

The servant scurried out of sight.

I looked away to the far line of cottonwoods adjacent to the depot building, and saw that Peter squatted behind the treeline, still watching the Pullman.

The gunman caught my gaze and followed it. "Sir," he said, grave and quick as he turned from me and moved to the carriage door.

"What?" barked my father.

"Out there," the Pinkerton said. "Is that man a local hire of yours?"

"How should I know? It's not my responsibility to engage them. Dammit, is he not familiar to you?"

"No," he said quietly, following Peter with the rifle sight. "And he's watching this car mighty close."

"Where are my other guards?"

"You had me send them away, sir," the Pink replied.

"Nonsense!"

"On Sunday, if you remember. You said the locals couldn't be trusted."

"And maybe you're not to be trusted either! Get out there now and dispose of him."

The man turned quickly and bolted toward the door, his jacket falling open to expose another pistol. His eyes dark as iron and flinty with anger, he paused in the doorway for his bowler and duster.

"Go!" my father shouted, and the detective pounded down the steel steps to the ground.

We watched him sprint across the railyard in Peter's direction, rifle in hand.

"He's a good man," my father said, "although not as meticulous as you might expect from the Pinkerton Detective Agency." He held an arm out over the walnut table and the broken warhorses, nodding to me in the glistening afternoon light. "It's over now, John. Let's make plans for Mexico."

He spoke with controlled grace, the vilest talent imaginable. He opened his eyes wide, waiting for me to acquiesce to Tampico, to the filthy rat cage of his industry. I stared at him, and realized I could not remember a single day when I'd felt pride. "And what could you possibly think might be over?" I asked calmly.

He sat on the velvet chair and leaned back, as though affronted, or pretending so. He put both hands on the decanter like to a pommel, leaned forward over it and pulled the glass plug from the top.

"That's a sweet hole," he sighed, winking. "And this is a fine drink. A man brings it to me each spring in great caskets. All the way from the Isle of Skye. I'll pour for you now."

I walked to the table and pushed the glass toward him.

He began to drizzle the drink into the crystal. "Some fine things you've never been able to scorn." He stopped the pour suddenly. "In fact, you always accepted the finest I offered, didn't you?"

I grabbed the heavy glass and hurled it to the floor where it merely thumped and rolled across the woolen pile. "You change the truth of every minute in your life, don't you?" I shouted. "It's all pretense with you, with a few thefts and murders mixed in for good measure!"

The blue veins at his temples swelled like thick worms scrolling down his skull, bulged and pulsing. Trickles of sweat rose across his forehead and dripped into the coarse hairs of his mustache. He gulped at the air, then leaned for a cigarette from the box on the table.

Turning to me, he snapped, "Light it for me, boy, and let's finish our Tampico business!"

I shook my head slowly and did not move to his side.

Leaning across the table to the tinderbox lighter, he turned the valve himself. A gentle flame escaped through the hydrogen, and my father, his face like cankered earth, sucked the tobacco deep into his chest. Suddenly, a single sharp crack from afar exploded through the air, and he jumped up and walked briskly to the carriage door.

"It seems our detective has finished his task," he said smiling. A soft boom rippled across the railyard.

I snatched the Remington from the table and ran to the door.

My father flung it open and stepped onto the platform, into a light, freezing rain. Scanning the freight boxes and the depot, I saw not a single soul shifting across the rails, until out of the rain came Peter, trudging through the mud, rifle and pistol in his hands.

My father reached back and pulled me forward. "There," he said. "He is the last of them. Go and finish this." Peter ducked behind a horse and its buggy, stooping low under the line of thick ebony wood siding. "You see? Olenbush is afraid. Nothing more than a parasite. When he comes round the carriage, shoot him!"

"I will not!" I cried, and I imagined my friend lying prone in the mud, his bones shattered and skin translucent in the dying light.

"Then give me my gun, boy. I'll have the end of him."

Turning a corner behind the buggy, Peter began to run toward us.

"Give me!" my father hissed. He held his hand out, index finger pointing straight in my face. "Give me that pistol!" he shouted. And then in a voice so low I might have dreamed it, he added, "You don't even have to go to Tampico. Just shoot him! Or give the gun over and let me do it." He lunged at me, and I stepped back into the car. "Half for me and half for you, son. It can belong to you immediately!"

"Never," I said. I lifted the Remington until its muzzle lined up with his heart. "I'll have you," I whispered, "for Daniel."

I pulled the trigger with the greatest care, slow and hard. The bullet exploded from the muzzle, cutting deep into his chest. The force knocked him backward off the platform onto the barleyweeds of the railyard, where he lay without moving.

I stepped down into the pools and the mud, bending over him to check for life. I observed his pupils for movement, and put my fingers preciously close to his mouth. I felt no breath cross his lips, and for a moment the wild grief frozen on his face gave me sweet pleasure.

CHAPTER 33

Peter knelt beside me in the jellied mud and stroked his thumbs down over my father's eyelids.

"I see we had the same thought, Johnny." He shoved his fingers into my father's jacket pockets, foraging about. "We both need to put ends to all this." He paused to wipe his hands on his pantlegs, and I saw it was blood he was cleaning away.

"Where's the Pink?" I asked.

"Layin' in the gray slime by the cottonwoods."

"You all right?" I pointed at his bloody trousers, but he only shrugged.

"Blood is all the same, ain't it? Mine or his, who knows?" He leaned over and took my father's handkerchief, wiping his palms again till the skin began to redden. "As long as we get to Stella and Rufus soon, I'll be fine." Grabbing his hat from his skull, he pushed his blond hair back off his forehead. His hands, hair, and cheeks alike, all of him glistened in the twilight with the silvery wet grime of that yard. "I'm guessin' there's no one left inside. We clear to leave?"

"Leave?" I asked slowly, still dazed by the smoky smell of the last bullet. Since the day I'd been sent west I'd watched the burial grounds growing, bodies appearing from nowhere at the edges of these graveyards, left to stink with all the others. Even my father now lay in mud marbled with his own blood. The gentle taps of more rain fell through the dark branches of the few cottonwoods that still stood outside the barbed wire. These taps grew harsher with the power of the downpour. "I can't possibly leave yet," I said. "It's my responsibility to tell Stella now."

"Tell her what?" he asked.

"Lucy was also murdered today. By my father and one of the marsh musicians, there in the railcar where they kept her a prisoner. The marshers were also in his employ."

Fearful as a child backed to a cold wall, Peter did not respond.

"They tortured her, burned her, then my father shot her," I continued. "Her corpse was dragged off by his servant, to the cemetery, probably. Or ditch-dumped somewhere closer. I need to find her and bury her properly. And explain it all to Stella."

"You'd tell Stella what happened to her sister just to get the truth outta your heart?" He wiped the back of his hand across his face, warily as though to ponder the taste of the night. "Just because you survived doesn't give ya the right. You got nothin' to say to her, John. Nothin' about Lucy that won't cause my girl pain."

And she was his girl. Never mine. An evening sparrow perched silently on a branch of a single cottonwood near the depot, both the bird and the tree the color of wintered stones. "Except she deserves to know, and knowing is a kind of end," I said. My voice was tired, my words hollowed out. "Don't we owe a respectful burial to Lucy? A gift to her miserable life."

"The woman's dead. Risking our lives to bury her ain't a gift. Savin' her mighta been, but it's a little late for that." His fingers curled around the pistol butt, his green eyes gone nearly black.

A far streetcar began to grind through town, the last one of the day before the new electric lamps lit the streets and the chili queens came to the plaza.

"Half a life ago I had hoped to make a home here," I said. "Build a school on the river maybe, look for some rough peace right here. But there's no peace, is there?"

The lighting began to glow at the corner of the depot building, and with that the noise of the city rose up those streets.

"Not anywhere, John, truth be told. Let's move your pa's body out of sight now, and then we can leave San Antonio once and for all."

I looked down at the carcass of Theophilus Ives, a man reviled by journalists and politicians, alike; by his sons, even, and prosecuted by his partners. With nuclein so universally loathed, I knew, as did the good Friar Mendel, I could never escape that blood.

A wood cart clattered in the distance; I shuddered, and hoped that my father's soul had left my commune. "Yes," I said, almost not recognizing the depth of my own voice. "Thank you."

"But we'll keep the killing of Lucy from her. Agree with that, my friend?" He frowned slightly, like a shaman honoring pain. "You saved my life. And I'll do the same for you, but it'll ruin Stella if she finds out what happened to her sister. And we must go quick. Make the Spofford train to California, so we can get out of Texas by Friday."

"Yes," I said again. I cocked my ear at a sound beyond the Pullman. "Did you hear that? The wind off the canal? Or maybe footsteps?"

"Naw, Johnny. Just a wagon. On its way to St Brigid's Cross, probably to catch wild hares for a soup." He propped the rifle against the car and stared at my father's corpse. "This'd be cause for a rosary in Bavaria, ya' know. Come on, then." Above us a band of dark plovers flew in silence, bound homeward. He looked across the body at me, and leaning over he lifted my father's shoulders, nodding to me to take the boots.

We dragged it beyond the tracks, undressed it, and tied rocks to his chest. We shoved him into the irrigation canal, watching his head and legs hit the ragged stone shelves on the way down the bank. The body splashed into the water, splattering my face as I peered into the darkness, and I realized this anointing would be his last act on the earth. We put his clothes into a small pile of twigs and lit them to burn, not leaving until the cloth had turned to char.

Far down the canal bank as we were, the night was utterly still but for Peter's harsh breathing as he labored to stand. Finally, he wiped the drops off his cheeks and asked, "You ready?"

I shook my head. "I'm sorry. I need to find Lucy and bury her. I can't go with you now; I can't simply leave her wherever the boy discarded her."

He stooped forward and climbed up the slope to the trail. High on the berm, he stamped the mud off his boots and pulled on a pair of old riding gloves, frayed and dark with sweat lines. "I guess you've considered what will happen if you're caught," he replied.

"Yes."

"I doubt you really have. Here, I'll go. I'll do it. I can be quick like you never could. Besides, Stella and her kin are my responsibility. You go on out the camino as far as the pecan grove. She'll be waitin' with Rufus. Stay there and keep 'em safe. I'll find the servant and get him to tell me what became of Lucy's body." Nodding to himself, he added, "Don't worry, Johnny."

By the time I reached the old Lipan road, I was beyond the new lights of the city, and all around me the night was blacker than a cave. I found Stella's camp on a palisade by the Medina in a copse of pecans. A lip of the wind pursed heavily on the ridge, while from behind the bare trees I heard her voice.

"Where've you men been?" She stepped round a thick trunk, casting light from a lantern she held. Clutching Rufus's hand in the beating rain, she strode toward us and I reined up abruptly. The wool dress she wore was the same she'd worn for days, once forest green like a hunter's clothing, but now collied with grime and water.

I slid to the ground and took the lantern from her. "Come here, Rufus," I said, and the boy walked to me. "Take my horse and tether it."

"Where's Peter?" Stella asked, her voice scarcely more than a scratched whisper. She pointed at me. "You've blood stains on your chest." I looked down the cotton to where she held a halo of lamplight and I felt my face flush. Even now, knowing she would soon marry my friend, even now, standing before her with knowledge that could wreck her, I adored her still.

"Peter is coming shortly. There was a little Pinkerton trouble, is all. He's fine and I'm fine." I gulped and out of decency, pressed hard on myself to believe these words. "We'll have to ride all night to reach Spofford Junction. Come, I'll help you pack the kit."

Stella set the lamp on the ground beside the dying fire, and kicked earth across the remaining flames. "You're certain Peter will come?"

"Of course." We heard a toad trilling loudly near the horse, and I could make out the heart-shaped shadow of the boy squatting near a pool. I grabbed blankets from the berm and handed them to her. "Rufus, let's get to work. Come help your mama."

He nodded without the smallest pause. When he stood alongside us, Stella handed him a small sleeping pad. "Roll this up, Rufus. We'll take it all the way to California."

He put it under one arm, and held his other hand out to us. There in his palm lay Lucy's carved coal coin, the soft light of the rising moon glinting across it.

"Found this in the toad pool," he said. "What is it?"

Stella tore it from his hand and flung it far into the trees where it fell into a pile of rotted leaves. "Nothing, Rufus," she said.

He began to run to retrieve it.

"It doesn't belong to you!" she called to him. "Leave it and come here now!" The child's mouth dropped open and his eyes glowed with misgiving.

"You don't really want to toss it away," I said calmly.

"You've no idea what I truly want, John," she said. "I want to be in California. I want to stop seeking a mad woman who's run away yet again. My own life, that's what I want. I want my life to start." She stopped abruptly, her cheeks red and heated with rising blood.

"Lucy was a sad girl, but not harmful. That piece is all you'll have of her, maybe ever."

Unmoving, Rufus remained at the edge of the pecan trees, watching her.

"Get back here, boy," she said, but her words were loud and low, a growling sound I'd never heard from her before. He took a sharp step back farther into the woods.

I walked to him, saw that he was trembling, and put my palm gently to him, flat on his back. "It's all right, Rufus," I whispered. "Here, give me your hand and I'll go with you." I bent beneath the bare branches as we walked, and he did as well, stooping slightly though unnecessarily for he was so small.

When we reached her side, she grabbed him from me. "Don't touch him!" She put one arm around him and pulled him against her waist. "He's not yours to hold."

I walked to the leaves, all of them rotting to gelatin. I dug through them until I felt the flat, round coal piece, slick with mold and damp. Staring so closely at the four letters carved into it, the rough curves of a skewered heart, I could smell the sweet scent of pecans.

"Come to me, Stella," I said, but she didn't move. So I walked to her side, took her hand, and put the coal on her soft palm. "I need to tell you some things."

CHAPTER 34

Stella did not speak for a long time. Even when we heard a horse's clops along the river trail, still she sat on a fallen log staring at the vein of frozen moss clinging to the bark. Rufus knelt beside her, tugging at her hand, and every so often he would whisper *Mama?* or *Miss?* trying hard to find her right name, the one that would allow him home again. But she gazed straight up at the sky, waiting without so much as a touch to the boy's collar.

When Peter pulled up the rise, she stood and approached him, careful to keep her eyes averted above his horse, above the treeline that hid the river from us.

"Packed up?" he asked, and slipped from the saddle. He planted his boots in the mud, but she said nothing. "Stella?" He leaned over her, close and warm, kissed her mouth, but her arms hung straight at her sides like a ragwoman's, her forehead bare and glowing.

I heard the creak of the harness, and the cracking of the horse's shod hooves on the rocks as the animal trod nervously for firmer ground.

"We're cold, is all," I said, but not even a buffoon would have believed me.

"What's wrong with her?" He turned to her again, took both her hands and pulled her round to face him. "Stella?" he asked, pressing his mustache against her lips, but her expression didn't change. "What did you do, Johnny?"

"Nothing," I said, and as I did, Stella pulled herself free from him, opened her fist, and displayed the piece of coal.

"He gave me this," she said, moving away from both of us. "It belonged to Lucy, and now I know."

Peter's mouth dropped open. His eyes widened, and he wheeled round to me. "What did you tell her?"

"Everything," Stella said evenly.

I stepped back, coiled back, and gasped. "It wasn't right to let her hate her sister because of a lie we concocted," I said quickly. "It's not fair to hide Lucy's truth."

The two of them stared at me while a hundred futures crumbled. In that moment, when the thin glow from the stars and the moon merged, when my friends stood opposite me in silence, that was the moment that I understood the true nature of the callow, futile truth, and having at last uncovered it, I had no one to tell.

Peter and I loaded the horses while Stella waited with Rufus in the pecan copse, cupping that coal coin in one of her small hands. We lifted the child and the woman behind us and rode hard through the night until we reached Spofford Junction. As we arrived, the winter sunlight, that first weak sunlight of the day, threw gauzy glow over the windows of the new station building.

"Stay with them," Peter said. "I'll get the tickets."

"Don't bother about mine. I'm not sure where I'll be going. Maybe Boston. Maybe Sacramento."

He pursed his lips without speaking.

"I'll get my own ticket," I said, tapping a silent tune with my fingertips against the tweed over my belly.

He shrugged. "Makes sense. We're not really your family." Turning quickly, he strode away across the haphazard planks of the new-built boardwalk.

I squatted beside Rufus, putting my hand on his scrawny, shivering shoulder. "You'll warm up when you get on the train. The sights you're going to see, boy. All the way to California! You won't believe your luck."

"Luck?" he asked, so softly. "I ain't never been lucky."

I brushed the lingering raindrops from his jacket and stood up to face Stella. From my pocket I pulled a thick, ivory card, the front printed with my name, *John Henry Ives*, and on the back, I had inked in my own precise handwriting the number and street of our company's legal representatives. "Here are people who will always know where I am," I said, but she didn't take it. I took one step back. I had lost her, or never had her; still, I wanted her never to forget me. "I'll always remember that baking white sun on the hotel veranda last summer, Stella. And how you made me whole again." Only then did she reach for my calling card and when she did, her fingertips brushed against mine. "If you need anything, send them a telegraph and they'll get it to me."

At first she nodded slightly, turning her shoulders to step away. Ruefully then, she fixed her eyes on me for just a moment before she took the child's hand. They walked to the station hut where Peter stood waiting for them, and Rufus raised his arm, waving to me.

"How will I find you?" I called out to Peter. "I mean, if ever I come west."

"I expect it won't be hard," he replied, but I never spoke to him again. In two years, he was dead of lung swelling, buried in the old Potter's Field cemetery on the east side of this city.

I headed to the Atlantic coast, carrying no valises, bringing with me no servants. I informed the car attendant that I required coffee and Frenchman's rolls, and he delivered these with a small pot of peach jam and butter, along with the *San Antonio Light*. I leaned back in a deep chair in the carriage drawing room without even opening the *Light,* and fell to sleep.

Three days later in New Orleans, a newsboy deposited a choice of week-old papers on the dining car tray, and I took from this the *New York Times*, drank my coffee, and read it slowly as though the glassy eastern sky where we were headed was heaven itself. I found buried on the fifth page of that issue a story of my father's unexplained disappearance.

By April, Theophilus Ives's involvement had been erased from every company's story, from every gentleman's club in Massachusetts and New York. Undeniably a worm of a memory, my father lost any veneration. I lingered on at Louisburg Square, engaging a detective out of the Thiel agency to seek Stella and perhaps a clue about what had become of Nora Nesbit, but he could find no trace. Through it all, I spent my days tying off the vestiges of my father's companies and accompanying my mother to her myriad medical meetings, praying for resolution, or at the very least, for a diagnosis.

Sometime in the early summer, Arcturus captured her whimsy, that red star glowing with war. More and more ragged, she asked me what became her last favor: the construction of a red granite obelisk, a small one, to my father's memory in our family section at the burying ground near the Boston waterfront. To this, I could only agree. That day, at the start of the Indian Summer, we dedicated it to him, but the attendance was pitiful, no family save the Vermont cousins, no business partners, and certainly not Gould.

After the ceremony, I put my mother in a hackney cab home, and wandered alone to the waterfront. To my astonishment, I saw my Thiel detective standing with a woman on the cobbled quay, both of them gazing straight into the salted September wind. When she saw me approaching, Nora Nesbit broke away from the man and rushed toward me, down the old fishing pier, throwing her head back in laughter, glittering with gratitude.

BEVERLY HILLS, 1926

The sunrise over this garden was better before we dug the oil wells along the coast. As today, when the light and the December heat lift through the sky, so does the stink of rock oil and old eggs. No matter how you gulp, smack your lips, or close your throat, no one escapes the acrid black honey under this land. That is the curse of Beverly Hills, and the reason why so many have moved even farther west to the beaches.

My empty whiskey bottle lies cracked on the path where I flung it an hour ago, intending to knock sense into my younger son who had just returned home. He still resides here on Maple Drive with us, and he came, three sheets to the wind, stumbling over my wild strawberries until finally he tripped flat onto them. He sat in the soil singing in his rich, drunk baritone, vocal cords that we once hoped would propel him to the opera, or at the very least, to that new Cocoanut Grove supper club.

"Shush, fool!" I shouted to him. "You'll be drawing your mother out before long!" Oddly, he stopped, or as my wife would say, he blacked out, and laid the side of his face against the dry December dirt.

Having regained the warmth of my morning, and before

Nora could put herself between me and my anniversary peace, I pulled a brittle yellow page from the pocket of my dressing gown. Once again, for the forty-second year, I began to read about the obscure truth of my father, a man who made millions, cheated so many, but whose disappearance was never explained.

ALSO BY ROCCIE HILL

The Blood of my Mother

A woman fights for her life as a refugee, slave, mother, and farmer, in this *"saga with many layers…[a] riveting, addictive journey"* (Joanne Hardy, author of *The Girl in the Butternut Dress*).

Acclaimed for her "wonderful" debut novel (*Publishers Weekly*), Roccie Hill, inspired by the story of her great-great-grandmother, now presents an unforgettable literary saga of a woman and a place, growing and enduring under multiple flags and through the sorrows and turbulence of history.

BUY NOW

ACKNOWLEDGMENTS

My thanks, as always, to my beta readers: Carmen Flores, Julie Starr, Mary Ann De Vlieg, Lynne Lockwood, Cathy Nolan, Teresa Robison Heine, and Kathie Flamm; to my dear writer's critique group: Patricial Ljutic, Joe Belden, John Fetto, and Andy Scontras because everyone should have such a sterling bunch behind them; to Joanne Hardy, who is my constant motivation to write the perfect word and do the right thing; and to my darling daughter, Nicky Polidor, who is the inspiration of my life. Thank you all for your belief in me, lo these many years.

A NOTE FROM THE PUBLISHER

Thank you for reading this book. If you enjoyed it please do consider leaving a review on Amazon to help others find it too.

We hate typos. All of our books have been rigorously edited and proofread, but sometimes mistakes do slip through. If you have spotted a typo, please do let us know and we can get it amended within hours.

info@bloodhoundbooks.com

A NOTE FROM THE PUBLISHER

Thank you for reading this book. If you enjoyed it please do consider leaving a review on Amazon to help others find it too.

We hate typos. All of our books have been rigorously edited and proofread, but sometimes mistakes do slip through. If you have spotted a typo, please do let us know and we can get it amended within hours.

info@bloodhoundbooks.com

9 781917 705073